# I'M NOT
# JULIA ROBERTS

# I'M NOT JULIA ROBERTS

$\bullet \quad \bullet \quad \bullet$

*Laura Ruby*

**WARNER BOOKS**

NEW YORK    BOSTON

This book is a work of fiction. Names, characters, places, and incidents are the product of the author's imagination or are used fictitiously. Any resemblance to actual events, locales, or persons, living or dead, is coincidental.

A variation of "Ballad of the Barbie Feet" first appeared in *The Florida Review* in 2003. A variation on "Picture of Health" appeared in *The Green Hills Literary Lantern* in 2004.

Warner Books
Hachette Book Group USA
1271 Avenue of the Americas
New York, NY 10020

Visit our Web site at www.HachetteBookGroupUSA.com.

Printed in the United States of America

First Edition: January 2007
10  9  8  7  6  5  4  3  2  1

Warner Books and the "W" logo are trademarks of Time Warner Inc. or an affiliated company. Used under license by Hachette Book Group USA, which is not affiliated with Time Warner Inc.

Library of Congress Cataloging-in-Publication Data

Ruby, Laura.
    I'm Not Julia Roberts / by Laura Ruby.
        p. cm.
    ISBN-13: 978-0-446-57874-5
    ISBN-10: 0-446-57874-6
    I. Title.
    PS3618.U234I15 2007
    813'.6—dc22                                    2006006832

*Book design by Giorgetta Bell McRee*

For Steve,
who keeps everyone straight

"I don't mind *him*," Mother said. She was excited, and she tipped her glass and spilled some gin into the sand. "I don't mind *him*. It doesn't matter how *rude* and *horrid* and *gloomy* he is, but what I can't bear are the faces of his wretched little children, those fabulously unhappy little children."

—JOHN CHEEVER
"Goodbye, My Brother"

• • •

"Harry, why does your generation always have to find the right person? Why can't you learn to live with the wrong person? Sooner or later, everyone's wrong."

—CHARLES BAXTER
"Fenstad's Mother"

# CONTENTS

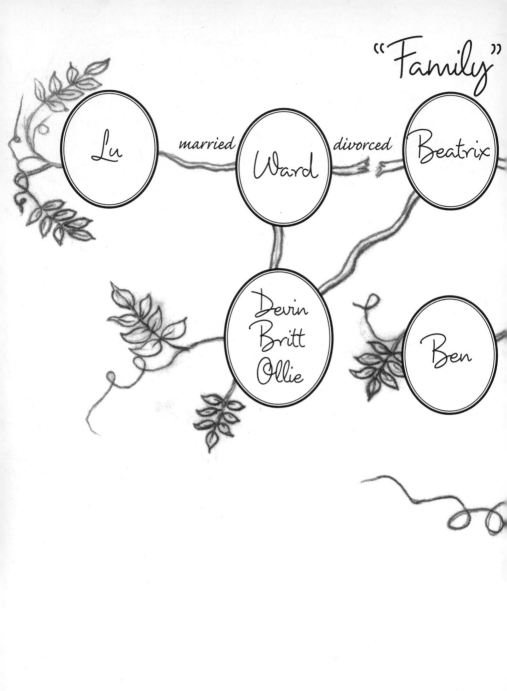

"Family"

Lu — married — Ward — divorced — Beatrix

Devin
Britt
Ollie

Ben

# Tree

married  **Alan**  divorced  **Roxie**

**Liv**

married  **Moira**  divorced  **Tate**

**Ashleigh Ryan**

**George**  married  **Glynn**

**Joey**  **Derek**

DATING

SIBLING TO

DIVORCED

# LIST OF CHARACTERS

Lu—a new stepmother
Ward—her husband
Beatrix—Ward's ex-wife
Devin, Britt, and Ollie—Beatrix and Ward's sons
Alan—Beatrix's second husband
Roxie—Alan's ex-wife
Liv—Alan and Roxie's daughter
Tate—Roxie's boyfriend
Moira—Tate's ex-wife and Roxie's friend
Ashleigh and Ryan—Tate and Moira's children
Ben—Moira's second husband
Glynn—Tate's sister and Moira's friend
Derek—Glynn's ex-husband
Joey—Tate and Glynn's son
George—Glynn's second husband

# I'M NOT
# JULIA ROBERTS

# LOOPY

Songs to accompany your life: "Heart like a Raisin"; "The Propeller Beneath My Wings"; "Time and Time Again in a Bottle"; "I Want to Smack Your Hand"; "Crazy."

The children were ugly. All scabbed knees and crooked teeth, lank ponytails and greasy bangs, stained purple mouths unhinged to the uvulas. They rushed at their parents and at one another, swinging heavy backpacks, pelting chalky pebbles, kicking out with their thick institutional shoes.

Lu stood away from the little clots of moms and the occasional dad, smoking a cigarette. She had quit some six months before, but when her husband told her that she would have to care for the boys all by herself for the week he was in Dallas, something thin and brittle inside her snapped. After four days with her nerves stretched colorless, smoking was the only thing keeping the cancerous thoughts from finding form on her tongue.

She smashed the butt under her boot while she eyed the school entrance, the endless stream of children draining from it. She watched as stout women in teddy bear sweatshirts tenderly clasped grape-sticky kids to their bosoms. Scraps of conversation floated around her.

"Britney had *three* hours of homework last night. What is with these teachers?"

"Is that the way you talk to me? Is it? You better watch that mouth!"

"I should be more patient with her. You know these Protestants, always going on about what the Bible says, as if anybody really knows. They don't even believe Mary is a saint."

Lupe Klein, neither Hispanic nor Jewish, raised a Lutheran, was tempted to say, "We don't believe *anyone's* a saint." But perhaps she was wrong. Perhaps, Lu told herself, these ugly children did beautiful, thoughtful, saintly things—splinted the broken wings of baby robins, tended to ailing grandmas and -pas, gave their last pennies to the poor. Perhaps she was too angry and shallow, too roiled with resentment, to see the beauty beneath the ugliness. Perhaps she was the wicked one.

In front of her, a tall boy plucked a knot of hair from the scalp of a smaller boy. The small one smacked a palm to his head and howled as the tall one waggled the knot, its tiny white roots quivering.

*Christ. We're all doomed.*

A woman standing next to her clucked her tongue. Lu

thought it was an unconscious comment on the hair pulling, but the woman said, "Sometimes they keep them."

*Who keeps who where?* "Excuse me?" Lu said.

The woman, who had spectacularly tidy hair, nodded toward the school doors. "Sometimes they keep certain classes after school. You know, if someone is pushing someone else in line, or something like that. There have been times I've waited ten or fifteen minutes."

"Oh," Lu said. "Right."

"I'm Glynn," the woman said.

Lu swallowed a sigh. "Lu."

"My son's in kindergarten. Afternoon session." Glynn smiled encouragingly, but Lu offered no more information. She had discovered very quickly that the word *stepmother* had a negative effect on most of the women in the school yard, and she was too fragile to risk a response. Lu wasn't sure what she would say if Ms. Tidy's face tightened, if it fell, if she said, *"Really?"* and leaned in, eager for the whole sordid story.

Lu was spared the small talk when Britt found her. He muttered a stiff, "Hi," through his glittering braces and trained his eyes on his own ankles.

"Hey, Britt," Lu said, her voice sounding peppy and false. "How was your day?"

"Stupid," he said. "Mrs. McGorney's an asshole."

Glynn and two other moms whipped around to stare, and Lu shot them a glare that was pure overcompensation. "A lot of people are," she said. "Most of the time you just have to put up with it."

Britt bobbed his head in a way that neither agreed nor disagreed, shrugged off his backpack just as Ollie waded through the throng of plaid skirts and wrinkled uniform trousers. As usual, he was crying, his upper lip blurred with snot. His untied shoelaces flapped.

"What now?" Britt growled under his breath.

Lu hushed him, though she had been thinking the same thing. She bent at the waist, bracing her hands on her knees. "What's the matter, Ollie?"

"I forgot my pencil case," he said, hiccuping through his tears. "My money was in it." Ollie was wide through the cheeks and soft through the body. The only thing pointed about him was his chin, which he worked silently in his grief.

Lu closed her eyes. A thousand questions coursed through her head, the answers to which, she knew, would only frustrate and annoy her. *Why did you take your money to school? Why did you put it in the pencil case? Why do you always insist on bringing things with you just so that you can leave them behind?* "How about we go back and get your pencil case?"

This just made Ollie cry harder. "We can't! They lock all the doors and you can't get back in!"

"Then you'll have to get your pencil case tomorrow." Lu moved behind him and hefted the thirty-pound pack off his shoulders so that he could stand up straight.

Ollie stamped his foot. "But what if my money gets stolen!"

"How can your money get stolen if no one can get back into the school, you freaking moron?" Britt said.

"Let's try to be civil, shall we?" Lu resisted, rather valiantly, she thought, the urge to smack Britt upside the head.

But the insult seemed to comfort Ollie somewhat, and he wiped his nose and cheeks with the back of his hand. "Can we go to school early tomorrow?" he said as they walked to the car. "So that I can be the first to go inside?"

"I think we can do that." At eight, Ollie still hadn't quite grasped the concept of time, and Lu was sure she could convince him that they were leaving early no matter what time they left. But then she was equally sure that as soon as he saw the line of children that had, inevitably, arrived before him, he would be flattened by a fresh wave of grief, and she would have to spend fifteen minutes consoling him before he would get out of the car.

Better to get up early.

Ollie's plump little hand tugged at her sleeve. "Ice cream?"

"I have soccer practice," Britt said, face suddenly tense with alarm.

"We can get ice cream and still get you to practice," Lu said. Ice cream was soothing and peace promoting. Ice cream was magical. Ice cream was something you could use later. *When you asked for ice cream, you got it. Now I'm asking you to put your dirty socks in the hamper.*

"But he eats so slow!" Britt said. "Practice starts at three-fifteen! And I still have to change!"

Ollie glowered. "I want ice cream."

"Mother fricking mother," said Britt, drawing more glares. "I just want to get to fricking practice!" He thrust both arms in front of him as if the boat were sinking and he had no choice but to swim for it.

Lu's tongue curled ominously around various threats, epithets, incantations, and she reached for her cigarettes.

"Loopy," said Ollie, releasing her sleeve and pinching his nose, "those make you smell."

They made it, just barely, to Britt's practice ("Fricking A, toad, will you stop dripping that fricking ice cream all over my fricking uniform?"). All Lu wanted to do was get Ollie set up with some puzzle books so that she could sit down on the couch, Picky a soothing bun in her lap. She had read somewhere that stroking pets for ten minutes a day could lower blood pressure. She wanted to work her fingers in Picky's tufted underbelly, unwind to his bumblebee buzzing, pet herself into a coma.

When they got back home, however, Devin was draped facedown across the couch, stupefied by MTV, and Picky was nowhere to be found.

Lu balanced an apple between Devin's shoulder blades, sure she could count his ribs right through his T-shirt. A few months before, he'd gone vegan. "Where's the cat?"

"Huh?" Devin did not take his eyes from the TV but deftly reached around and retrieved the apple, shined it on the couch cushion.

"My cat, Devin. Where's my cat?"

"Dunno," he said. "Around."

Lu could feel the thump of bass drums in her feet. "Did you forget to turn off the stereo downstairs?"

"Shoop's down there."

"Shoop?"

"Yeah, Shoop."

Lu dragged a hand through her snarled hair, pulling on it

painfully. When she was single, she never had knots. "Don't you think you should join him?"

"He's okay." Devin's eyes narrowed, and Lu turned to the TV, only to see a teen Barbie look-alike—openmouthed and glistening with sweat—grinding her hips at the camera. She wore her tiny pink panties *over* her jeans. Lu blinked. Were girls wearing their panties that way now? Had she been so traumatized by the transition from hip chick to mother hen that she hadn't noticed that underwear was no longer under anything?

"Hey, Dev, what the fuck . . ." A pale and shaggy boy about Devin's age stood in the doorway to the family room, scratching at his scalp. "Oh, sorry. I didn't know anyone else was here." Lu was relieved to recognize his look: psycho-punk with a Gen-Z edge. Long shaggy hair, tight black pants, and an eyebrow ring.

"Devin, why don't you go downstairs with your friend?" Lu pointed to the soda cans, paper plates, sneakers, and other assorted litter, the slime trails of teenagers. "I'd like to make this room more habitable for humans." She put her hands on her hips, going for authoritative yet cool. "And please, guys, the language? I'd like to see if I can keep Ollie from swearing like a rap star before he's ten."

Devin grunted and slid off the couch, grabbing one of the cans. The two boys stomped down the stairs to the basement, their reedy, warbling voices wafting up.

"Who's the chick?"

"Stepmother."

"She's all right. You think she'd do me?"

·    ·    ·

What the cat loves: the smell of Ward's shoes, nail files, bathtubs, laser pointers, shrimp.

What the cat hates: vacuum cleaners, thunder and lightning, the tang of citrus, driving to the vet, big dogs, boys.


When they were little, they were adorable.

"Devin, Britt, and Ollie," Ward had said that first date, unraveling the ready strip of photographs that all dads tote around. They were twelve, ten, and five, respectively.

"Devin, Britt, and Ollie," Lu repeated. Whatever happened to Mike? Or John? Images of an old puppet show she had seen when she was a kid bounced through her thoughts. *Kukla, Fran and Ollie.*

She lifted the strip of photographs. "Kukla," she said.

"What?"

"Cute. *Cute.*"

The boys were small, doe eyed, and elfin featured. Someone, their mother, Lu supposed, had coaxed each boy's thick dark hair into sweet curls that would have undone Bill Sikes and Fagin alike. Ward saw them one evening a week and on weekends. Easy enough, he told Lu, because right after the divorce he had bought a house just a few blocks from the ex and her new husband. "The boys can just walk over."

"Great!" said Lu, lighting a cigarette in a toast to conveniently located ex-wives. Her mother had warned her against dating divorced men, but Lu was in her mid-thirties and had just moved back to the Midwest. Who the hell else was she going to date?

To her surprise, her first meeting with the kids was so

pleasantly uneventful that Lu was soon dining with Ward and his children every Wednesday, dropping by every weekend. Unlike some of the horror stories she'd heard, the boys were always polite to her, never calling her rude names, never dismissing her out of loyalty to their mother. Of course, during their longer weekend visits, Lu was often out showing shockingly overpriced condos to wealthy people, but still, those brief visitations were comfortable and reliable as a Volvo.

Then one evening—three years after they met, five months after their wedding, twelve hours after they bid on a Tudor just fifteen minutes away in historic Oak Park—the bell rang and Lu opened the door to find Devin and all of his belongings on the porch, his mother's car peeling away from the curb. "Devin's all settled in high school now," Ward said. "How can I ask him to switch, leave all his friends? That would just upset him more than he is already."

"He stares at my breasts, Ward."

"It's only for a few years."

"I could be dead in a few years."

It seemed to Lu that Devin had turned from an elf to a monosyllabic troll overnight. Something heavy and damp and odorous that the ex had thrown off like an old coat in a hot spell. And that wasn't all she threw off. In a long and detailed letter sent with the boy, the ex announced that she could no longer take Britt to the orthodontist, citing scheduling conflicts with that office, and could no longer support Ollie's psychotherapy, citing philosophical conflicts with modern psychology. Then there were the half days, vacation days, parent-teacher conferences, soccer practices, and sick days from school that she thought Ward could handle. Or perhaps Lu could help with? "I understand," she wrote, "that a real estate agent's hours are quite flexible."

"Let me guess. Ontological conflicts with the concept of childhood? Theoretical conflicts with the idea of responsibility?"

"She has to work, Lu." The ex was marketing director at Heartland's Best Foods, maker of Ollie's brand wheat bread. Lu wondered which had come first, the boy or the bread.

"And what am I? Chopped liver?" Lu said. "I am, aren't I. Lu's Best Liver."

"Come on, Lu. I'll take care of most of it."

Most of it? The note had also mentioned that Britt's history project—a diorama on the Crusades—was due on Tuesday, and he still hadn't gone to the library. Lu's hysteria mounted, and she could feel a pulse in her eyeballs. "There's nothing like a little Loopy Liver to liven up your life!"

"What am I supposed to do? I called. I discussed. I yelled. They're my kids, Lu. Tell me what choice I have."

She stood there in the cramped kitchen, holding a bunch of mismatched silverware that she had been planning to give to Goodwill, and wondered how she could have been so thoroughly duped.

Her eyeballs kept her up at night, thrumming away into the dawn.


Ollie was perched at the kitchen table, delicately licking his ice-cream cone. He ate so slowly, it had melted all over his hand.

"Ollie, did you see the cat anywhere?"

"Stevie said a cat had babies under his porch. There are twenty babies. They don't have any eyes."

"I meant Picky. Did you see Picky?"

Ollie made a face. "I saw him drinking out of the toilet bowl this morning. Why does he do that? It's gross."

"Yeah, well, you pick your nose. That's gross, too."

"I do not pick my nose!"

Lu gave him a look and a napkin.

Picky, short for Piccolo, was a little gray pelt of a thing, a tiny scrap of biology that Lu had found huddled in the bottom of a garbage can at a New York City apartment building, back in her other life. He had stopped growing at six months, retaining the size and energy of an adolescent. Though he was close to seven years old, Lu still had to pluck him from the top of the screen door, where he often got stuck, splayed like a science experiment.

Picky was a living retreat for Lu, a handful of calming noises and familiar smells (his fur was loamy and sweet, like beets). When she got home from work, Picky would methodically clean each of her fingertips with his tongue, sanding away the limp handshakes, defiant keys, strange doorknobs, and stained countertops. And in this crowded house full of increasingly unfamiliar activities, loud noises, and unanticipated demands, Picky reminded her who she had been. Or at least reminded her that she *had* been someone else once.

When she first moved in, Ward complained of a slight allergy to cats; for Christmas, Lu had wrapped an economy-size package of Benadryl.

Lu opened the linen closet in the hallway, shoving aside

shampoo bottles to peer behind them. One time, Picky had been trapped in that closet all day, and he'd been forced to pee in the bath towels. When she finally found him, he'd run from the closet, his harsh birdlike squawks berating her for her neglect.

Now, Lu neatly stacked the piles of towels on the floor, then gave up and started yanking them out and tossing them over her shoulder. No Picky, but under the stacks, stuck in a corner, a single envelope gone yellow with age.

"What's that?" Ollie wanted to know.

"Not sure," said Lu. She opened the envelope. Inside was an old Polaroid of the ex. Wearing only a nightie and panties. Hugely, majestically pregnant.

"What is it?" Ollie repeated. "Can I see?"

The ex stood there staring down at herself, her gauzy baby doll pulled up to reveal a basketball-size tummy, expression somewhere between pride and bewilderment. She couldn't have been more than twenty-five, just a kid herself, beautiful in that way the young are, smooth and white and firm.

*She looks like a doll,* thought Lu. *If dolls came knocked up.*

"Loopy!" said Ollie, whining now. "Let me see!"

"Nothing to see," said Lu, cramming the photo in her pocket. "People you don't know."

Ollie's face had gone red and crumpled. "But I want—"

"Not now, Ollie. I'm trying to find Picky." Lu dropped to her knees to dig through a jumble of old bath toys stowed on the last shelf. Who'd saved that picture? And what, exactly, was a person supposed to think about it? It was almost repulsive in its intimacy, in its careless, youthful sexiness. Was it a reminder? A lament?

Lu pulled out a plastic pony with ratted pink hair. "Where the hell could that cat be?"

Ollie, scowling, thwarted: "You're not supposed to say H-E-double-toothpicks in front of children."


Britt slammed into the house, trudging in dirt as well as major attitude. Lu was crawling around on the floor, looking for Picky under benches and footstools, the little tents made by the newspapers. Britt behaved as if Lu's posture were normal.

"Fricking coach benched me," he said, throwing open the refrigerator door.

Lu looked up from the newspapers. She could hear the rustle of plastic wrap and knew that when she checked later, she would find every leftover container open and a fingerful of the contents missing. "Why did he bench you?"

"How am I supposed to know why he benched me? He just benched me."

Lu might have been more sympathetic had Britt not said something similar when he was suspended and nearly expelled from school a few months back. He had neglected to mention that he'd been caught stuffing copies of *Playgirl* into the desk of Mrs. Rubens, his English teacher. "I thought it would help her out," he'd claimed, unfazed.

Britt slammed the fridge door shut, thought better of it, opened it again. "Fricking Mom didn't even come to the game."

"Isn't fricking Mom still away?"

"What else is new?"

She thought of the photograph in her pocket and opened

her mouth to defend the woman, then snapped it shut. Though she had found the ex a bit erratic and self-absorbed, she had made it a point to not have much quarrel with her. Until Devin showed up with his pillow, Ollie with his night terrors, and Britt with endless unfinished dioramas. Until Ward had announced his business trip in Dallas and the ex immediately hopped a junket to Vegas.

The ex had, in the last few years, grown progressively larger and, Lu believed, shorter. To her surprise, Lu was not pleased by the ex's new bulk, her newly hatched jowls, the burgeoning buttocks, the downturned mouth creasing the fleshy face. The bulk just made the woman all the more solid, more formidable. Self-contained. Unmovable. Her face jutted out from her body like the prow of an ancient warship.

Lu hated her the way she'd hated her own mother years before, with a desperate, ineffectual, shrieky passion that bordered on adolescent.

Bordered? *Ha!* Prolonged exposure to the first wife caused emotional regression in the second, she was sure. Someone should study this. Soon she'd be sucking her thumb and screaming for a rattle.

But worse than hating the ex was that Lu had started to hate Ward for having married the woman some gazillion years before, for having chosen such a solipsistic person as a mate. What could that say about *him*? And then what did marrying Ward, choosing someone with such flawed taste, say about Lu herself?

There they were, the whole ahistorical, solipsistic lot of them, twirling pell-mell around their own universes like planets without suns. Not a grown-up in the bunch.

She threw the papers back to the floor. "Britt, have you seen the cat?"

He took out the milk, unscrewed the cap, and lifted the jug to his lips. "I just fricking got here."

Where the cat wasn't: in the cabinets or in the windows, under the beds or in the bathtubs. Not in the closets, dresser drawers, hampers, or bookshelves.

The basement ceiling, where several tiles had been punched from their metal fasteners and strewn about the floor. Lu looked up into the yawning hole and watched for furtive movements in the dark.

After Ollie finished his ice cream, he remembered the money irretrievably stowed in his pencil case and was swept away in a fresh wave of melancholy.

"It's okay, Ollie. We're going to leave early tomorrow, re-member? You'll get your money first thing. Now, how about another puzzle? This looks like a good one. . . . No? Do you want to play a game of cards?"

She felt a headache brewing in the back of her neck. Who would have known there were so many things to confront? Half-naked exes. Her patience gone missing. Her heart, dull as a fist.

Lu plunked the weeping Ollie in front of the TV and sneaked into the bathroom with the cordless phone and her cigarettes.

Lu's sister, Annika, answered after fourteen rings. Because of some potent fertility drugs, Annika had one more moon-eyed baby than she had arms. Lu had stayed with Annika for those first chaotic weeks after the births and had found herself reeling around in a sympathetic mommy-fog for almost a month afterward. The sheer physical demands of her infant nieces had astonished and then terrified her. In comparison, Lu's own complaints seemed about as consequential as a $25 parking ticket. Still, Lu didn't know who else to call, who else wouldn't hold it against her.

"Talk to me," said Annika. Her tone was chipper, but her voice was ragged with exhaustion.

"Devin's holed up in the basement with a boy named Shoop, probably scouting for porn on the Internet, Ollie's sobbing in front of *SpongeBob SquarePants,* and Britt has to build a model of an Incan village by tomorrow."

"Sounds like fun," said Annika. "I'd join you, but I have an appointment to get my fingernails pulled."

"And I can't find Picky anywhere."

"I'm sure he's just hiding. And can you blame him?"

"No, I guess not," Lu said. "Listen to me whine about myself. How are you?"

"How am I? Who am I? Who's this 'I' that people keep talking about?"

"That doesn't sound good," Lu said.

Annika half coughed, half sighed into the phone. "Oh, they're good. Good babies. Really. You know, they *do* sleep occasionally, and that's something. It's just that there are so very *many* of them. Thank God for the nanny. I'm obsessed with this nanny."

"When did you get a nanny?"

"I didn't tell you? I broke down and hired her a few days ago. Her name is Jewel, like the singer."

"Does she sing?"

"No, but she can diaper a wriggling baby with one hand tied behind her back." She sighed. "At least I have girls. At least girls don't pee on you."

Lu found herself saying, "Yeah, but girls have that period between eight and ten where their heads have grown to adult size but their bodies haven't. You have to keep scrubbing the lip gloss off of them because it's too damned disconcerting. Every girl in Ollie's class looks like something out of a Victorian painting." She winced, though Annika couldn't see it. Why did she have to say stuff like this?

"That won't happen for at least seven years," Annika said. "By then, they'll have some nice drugs that can take the edge off, but won't upset your stomach."

"There's always cyanide."

"Jesus. What's going on over there?"

"Never mind. I can't even talk about it. When I do, people look at me like I'm dangerous."

"They're afraid you're going to gather up your stepkids and drown them like a litter of kittens. I mean, we're a reductive people. No genetic investment, no real investment."

Lu could almost see her sister with an invisible cigar, waggling her brows: *Hey, Snow White, ever been to the woods?* She looked at herself in the bathroom mirror, face drawn, cigarette cocked, frowned at the image. "They need so much, Annie. It's not like the babies. It's different. They can feed themselves and dress themselves, but all they have to do is *stand* there and you can see how much they need. And I'm such a moron that I didn't think about that part."

"Of course you didn't think. If we actually thought about anything, who'd get on a plane? Who would have sex? Who would have their nipples pierced?" Annika's voice took on a slightly hysterical edge. "And, not that I'm the best example right now, damn it to hell, but where's their mother?"

"Their mother is molting. And she's just getting bigger and stronger and freer. You should see her. She looks like a giant bird. Like a great white bird in a blue business suit."

"She's a bitch and I hate her."

Lu dropped her cigarette in the toilet and watched it float round and round. "We all do."

"I mean it, Lu, I totally fucking hate her."

Lu could hear a snuffling sound, and she marveled again at the self-absorption that had prompted her to call Annika, whose ruined belly looked like the smirking face of a very old man.

"I'm sorry, Annie. I wasn't thinking."

"Oh, fuck it," Annika said. "Fuck, fuck, fuck! I'm going to keep saying it, because I'm sure as hell never doing it again."

"I shouldn't have called."

"Yes, you should. You have to." More snuffling. "I need to know there are other women out there in the world so tired they've forgotten their own names. Do you know what your name is?"

"I think it's Jennifer," said Lu.

"There you go," Annika said.

Lu cleared her throat, adopted the breezy tone of a sitcom mom. "It gets a little worse."

"It better," Annika barked. "This is my sanity we're talking about."

"You know that mole under my nose?"

"Yeah?"

"I have a hair growing out of it."

"Thank God."

Lu squeezed her eyes shut and listened to Annika breathe. "Well. I suppose I should start thinking about the Incas now since I'm pretty sure Britt hasn't."

"Incas. I'll add that to my list," said Annika. "Learn to diaper babies one-handed, learn to function on 2.3 hours of sleep per night, become expert on Incas. What the hell do you know about the Incas?"

"I know that they were into human sacrifice," Lu said.

"Ha! Who isn't?"


Renaming the dwarves: Itchy, Sticky, Snotty, Grubby, Mouthy, Truculent, Deliberately Obtuse.


It was Britt who had gifted her with the name "Loopy."

At ten, he was like an amiable dog, eager to get in any car for any reason. Lu often took him along when she ran errands. One Saturday, they went to the bank. He watched as Lu signed all her checks, sounding out her full name. He pronounced it "Loop."

"No, Britt. It's Lupe. Lu-pay."

"Loopy?" he said, and giggled. "Loopy! What kind of name is that?"

She could endure the brattiness of her richest clients but was always unprepared for the bluntness of grade schoolers. "Well, what kind of name is Britt?" Lu said, childishly imitating his tone.

"My grandfather's name."

"Oh." Lu scratched at the bottom of her bag for a deposit slip. "My mother's name is Sue, and her sister's name is Jane. She got a little inventive when she had her own children. Just call me Lu. It's easier."

He thought a moment. "I like Loopy."

This was at a time when all the people and all the books cautioned her to allow potential stepchildren to call her what they liked, to bestow their own special titles. She had been hoping for something a bit more dignified, not a name that, when written, encouraged a person to fill the double o's with little cross-eyed pupils.

"How about Lulu?" she suggested.

"I like Loopy."

"Luna? That's 'moon' in Italian."

"Loopy," he said. Without warning, he began to wave his arms around and jog in a circle, a cross between a rain dance and a celebration of the Chinese New Year. Startled and embarrassed, Lu tossed furtive glances at the other patrons as Britt chanted her new name: "Loo-PEE, Loo-PEE, Loop-PEE . . ."


She plucked the hair from her mole and then all of the other stray hairs that seemed to be sprouting randomly from her skin, then realized that dinnertime was approaching and, in her yearning for her cat, she hadn't given a thought to it.

Britt would eat anything sweet in any combination. Honey ham and carrots, a big hunk of cornbread. Twinkies with a side of peas that he would devour in a few huge, desperate bites.

Kid comfort food for Ollie. A hot dog or macaroni and

cheese that he would throw up at two in the morning after some nightmare featuring giant sharks with wings or flaky-faced crazy people. He would poke her arm in the middle of the night and tell her that the crazy people were angry again, plucking at him with their crazy fingers.

Devin would declare a staggering, gut-wrenching hunger and leave his meatless meal untouched.

She sighed, trying to remember if she had been as un-balanced as her stepchildren when she was young. She thought not, but what did she really know? Her mother told her that she used to cozy up to complete strangers at the grocery store, helping elderly women pick out peaches, chatting with the suburban moms. This bizarre friendli-ness, her mother said, stopped after the divorce. "That's when you got all stiff and strange and wouldn't talk to any-body."

That's it, Lu thought, dinner could wait. She threw open the bathroom door, walked down the hallway, and attacked Ward's closet. Maybe Picky had gotten in there somehow; she'd looked everywhere else. She knelt, tossing shoes over her shoulder, feeling along the floor way in the back.

The doorbell rang. Cursing, she stood and kicked the pile of shoes. Then she ran downstairs.

"Doorbell," said Ollie from his perch on the couch, glassy eyes glued to the cartoons.

"Really?" Lu said. It was probably for Ollie, too, or for Britt. Living with kids meant that the doorbell was always ringing, and there was always somebody who wanted to come in, small and medium-size somebodies who were in-variably hungry and thirsty and would need cheese sand-wiches or some Kool-Aid or new batteries for the

remote-control car, somebodies who scoured the house looking for the cat only to chase him under the bed.

She opened the door. A man who looked vaguely familiar
stood there, grinning toothily. He was wearing a brown suit
and carrying a dark red briefcase.

"Yes?" Lu said.

"Lu!" said the man, still grinning.

"Yes," Lu said again, trying to place him. One of the kids'
friends' parents? One of the neighbors? She was adrift in a
sea of faces. She could never keep all of them straight.

"It's Mike," said the man. "Mike Ritchie. I'm a friend of
Alan's."

Lu blinked. "Alan?"

"Beatrix's husband," said the man with the red briefcase.
"She told me that you might be interested in an opportunity." He eyed the screen door as if Lu were supposed to
open it.

Lu could feel her left eye begin to twitch. "I'm sorry, did
you say that Beatrix sent you?" Beatrix was Ward's ex-wife.

The man shifted his briefcase from one hand to the other.
"Beatrix and Alan work for me. As distributors for Energet-
ics? I'm sure you've heard of us. We're one of the top manu-
facturers of health care products."

"But Beatrix works for a food company," Lu said dumbly.
She knew about the whole pyramid scheme, of course, and
where Beatrix met Alan, but what did that have to do with
Lu? What was this man doing here, on her doorstep, swinging his red briefcase?

"It's pretty much Alan's business, but Beatrix helps out,"
the man said.

"Helps out. Okay," Lu said. Her face was heating up, and

she wondered if the man could see the flush rising in a pink wave across her cheeks.

"Now, I know that you sell real estate. Are you happy with that?"

"Happy?" Lu managed. "Yeah."

"Ah," said the man, Mike. "But not *really* happy."

Who the hell was *really* happy? "I'm doing just fine."

"But is fine enough?" said the man. "It's a choice."

"What's a choice?"

"What you do with your life."

Lu took a deep breath, suddenly so furious that her vision blurred around the edges. Wasn't it enough that evidence of Beatrix was everywhere, in the children, in the photographs, all through the house? Did the ex really need to send envoys, too, these grinning dispatches from a distant empire? "I don't think I'm interested in what you're selling."

The man's grin grew even wider. "But that's the beauty of it," he said. "I'm not selling anything but opportunity."

*If he says something about opportunity knocking, I will commit ritual suicide, right here, right now.* "I have a job. I like my job. I don't want to do anything else."

"You don't want to make up to two thousand extra a month, part-time?" said the man. "I have to tell ya, not many people would want to miss that." He held up his hand, palm facing the sky, as if holding out an invisible offering.

"I guess I'm one of the not many people," she said, now grinning herself, the way a bear would grin, baring its teeth.

Lu could see the man struggling not to tell her off. He was that type, she knew, the telling-people-off type, the kind of person who would get mad if someone didn't like the same movies he did. "Well," said the man, "it's your choice."

"Yes, it is," she said brightly.

He bristled at her tone. "The next time your boss comes down on you, don't say that opportunity didn't come knocking."

She opened the screen door. "I would never go around knocking on people's doors and pretend to be opportunity personified, okay?"

"Yeah, whatever, lady," said the man, his plastic smile gone, turning to leave.

"*Whatever?*" Lu shouted. "You come here, invading *my* house, wasting *my* time, and then you say *whatever* when I don't like it? Who the hell do you think you are?" She wanted to kick the man down the stairs.

"Nobody's invading nothing," said the man. "Christ. Have you been drinking or something?"

"No, but that's a good idea," said Lu. "Now get off my goddamn porch."


Britt didn't want to build the Incan village out of papier-mâché.

"Is this a philosophical or aesthetic problem?" Lu said, mostly to herself. She had splashed cool water on her face to calm down after the salesman left, but she was still breathing like an asthmatic.

"I want to build it out of Styrofoam," Britt said. "Don't they sell it at the crafts place? That place where we got the stuff for Babylon?"

"It's six o'clock already. We don't have time to go to the crafts store."

"This fricking sucks, man!"

"Yeah," said Lu. "It does. That's why I asked you to start the project a month ago, when it was assigned. And reminded you about it every day this week."

Britt rolled his eyes but said nothing, threw himself into a kitchen chair like an anchor into the sea. Devin shambled in, looking sly and pleased and secretive. Lu could only imagine what sexual mysteries he had cleared up for himself that afternoon.

"What's for dinner, Loop?" he said.

"Whatever you can scrounge up," Lu replied, wondering why he even bothered to ask. "I'm not doing anything until I find Picky."

"Well," said Devin, putting his hands on his hips just the way Lu always did, "where did you put him last?"

"Funny," said Lu, surprised by the unusual display of personality.

Devin snorted. "Maybe he got out."

"What do you mean?" said Lu. "Got out?"

"It's possible, Loop-la-loop," Britt said, braces flashing. "He was always looking out the screen door. He could have run away when we were leaving this morning. Or coming back this afternoon." He leafed through his notebook. "For all we know, he's in Indiana by now."

"Or Iowa."

"California. If I was a cat," said Britt, "that's where I'd go. Live outside all year round."

"You'd go anywhere." Devin pulled a box of cereal from a cabinet, keeping up appearances. "You'd go to Boise."

Lu turned and looked out through the window into the yard, everything dark and matted and slick from a cold, wet spring. Picky, *gone*? She scanned the bushes and the trees for movement, shaking her head, astonished by this new possibility, and then astonished at her own astonishment. It had never occurred to her that he might not turn up, her talisman against despair. She had never really believed that a life, even a small one, could be wiped out so quickly, so cleanly, like a spill.

"Come on," she said.

Britt closed the notebook. "Where are we going?"

"Help me, damn it!" Lu opened the back door and ran outside. "Picky!" she yelled. "Picky!" She ran around the yard like a dog on a line, circling, circling.

She could see Devin and Britt silhouetted in the doorway, watching her disintegrate with a queer sort of disaffection, as if this were precisely what they'd expected to happen, as if it were only a matter of time. It was Ollie who slid between them, opened the door, and sat on the porch steps, watching her ragged run slow to a jog, then a walk. She shuffled over and sat next to him on the steps, sucking wind. He waited until her breathing slowed, until she had wiped away the hot tears that had etched paths down her cheeks.

Ollie's damp fingers entwined with hers. "I'm sorry about Picky."

"Me too."

"Did you look in the toilet?"

Lu inhaled so swiftly that she gave a lame whistle, like a cooling teapot. "That's where I'll look next."

"Okay. I'll look with you. When you want to."

She gave Ollie's fingers a squeeze, feeling her own chin work at a hoary grief she wasn't sure she had a right to. She looked around the yard, trying to be brave, to see it for

what it was. But instead she pictured Peru in the days before the Spanish: the cities blazing with gold, the Inca
lying with his favorite wife, and the maiden slouching toward the temple—the girl assigned to keep this sunny
world safe.

# RESTORATION

Beatrix loves home improvement stores. The rows of ladders, the rolls of insulation, the stacks of wood, the smell of sawdust and machine oil and metal filings, the tools enshrined in their own special room—all of it fills her with a strange sort of joy, the sense of possibility.

This is a new thing. When she was married to Ward, she hated home improvement stores and all the dirty boys who flocked to them, hands palsied and eyes wild as they lingered over the drill bits, the tubing, the nail guns. But with Alan, a trip to the home improvement store—like a trip to the grocery store, fruit stand, dentist, park, or any other place— is different. Alan, as dirty as the rest of them when he's in the middle of a project, is as careful as those other men are crazed. When he reaches out to pull a box of screws from the shelves, Beatrix can see the authority in his movements, understands that he knows exactly how to use the equipment he selects. With Alan, she doesn't worry that he will pull the bathroom sink off the wall and leave it that way for the next year and a half. She doesn't fear that the washing machine he installed himself will suddenly and without warning vomit up gallons of soapy water onto the basement floor.

For Beatrix, the home improvement store has become a place where one sees one's future and buys the materials with which to build it. Beatrix pulls her hair into a ponytail, dons her overalls, and feels young and uncomplicated and adorable.

Today, they are shopping for paint. They have a pillow from their new couch, and they're trying to select the right color for the walls. There's just one problem. Well, two.

"You're going to paint it red?" says Problem One. "Walls are not red. *Meat* is red."

"Whatever," says Problem Two.

Problem One is small, thin, and perfect, long dark hair shiny and straight, smoky eyes glittering with contempt. She hates red. Pink reminds her of the insides of mouths. Beige is the color of an old man's teeth. Purple makes her want to puke. Yellow, she says, yellow is so over it's o-*ver.*

Problem Two is also thin, but shaggy haired, tall, and lanky, his arms hanging off his shoulders at odd angles like the limbs of paper dolls. Two doesn't speak much, and when he does, it is to express his utter lack of concern for home improvement and the middle-aged couples who value it.

Beatrix and Alan are standing in front of the Glidden paint display, holding the color swatches against the new pillow. It's the beginning of Memorial Day weekend, the ideal weekend for a project such as this one. The living room is already prepared—washed and spackled and sanded. They have to buy painter's tape, some tarps, new brushes, and the paint itself. It should have been simple, it should have been a pleasure, it should have been one of those mornings that Beatrix would recount to her incredulous friends: "I know! The hardware store! I haven't had so much fun since we went to get the new tires!"

But Beatrix hasn't counted on Liv, Alan's only child, and Devin, her oldest son, the two of them taking truculence to new depths. Though they are not exactly Pollyannas, Beatrix and Alan do believe in the power of teamwork, believe that something like painting a room can instill group pride and positive feelings. But so far, the Problems are interested only in being bigger problems. The two of them stand as far away from each other and from their respective parents as they can while still remaining in the same aisle.

"What do you think of this?" Beatrix asks, holding up a swatch of green, more sage than moss.

In response, Problem Two lifts his T-shirt and examines his rippled abdomen.

"It's nice," Problem One offers, "if you like snot."

"You're the snot," Alan says mildly. Beatrix believes she detects a hint of fondness in his voice and is once again amazed at his ability to remain sanguine around his daughter, who she believes would inspire thoughts of homicide in the pope.

"Alan," Beatrix says, "what do you think?"

He looks at the swatch. "I think it's green."

"But do you like it?"

Materials, Alan cares about. Colors, not so much. "Do *you* like it?"

"Of all that we've looked at, this matches best," Beatrix says, tapping the green swatch with her fingernail.

"Snot. Mucus. Phlegm," says One, pronouncing the "g."

Beatrix tries to ignore her. "I like this one."

"Just pick a color so we can get out of here," Two mumbles.

One tosses her hair. "You cannot like that color."

"I do," says Beatrix. "Amazingly enough."

"That's the thing," One says, nibbling thoughtfully at a hangnail. "It's not amazing at all."


Alan is methodical about taping before a paint job. Okay, he's downright anal, but that is, Beatrix knows, the only way to get the job done right the first time. These are things she wishes she'd understood when she was younger: details, follow-through.

"Remember the sides of the windowsill, Beatrix. You can take smaller bits of the tape and piece them together so that you get the right shape."

Beatrix rips off a shred of the brown tape, keeping an eye on the Problems. Problem Two is taping crookedly along the moldings in a way that will drive Alan nuts, though he won't comment on it. Problem One, who is supposed to be taping, is obsessed with the paint she disdains, stirring it over and over again, like a witch over a cauldron.

"Hey!" Alan says. "Are you helping or what?"

"I'm mixing."

"You're done mixing. How about some taping. The doorway, okay?"

Problem One heaves one of her impressive sighs, grabs a

roll of tape, and goes to the doorway. She holds the ring of tape in both hands like a crown and considers the door, as if someone infinitely more interesting—say, Prince William— were about to waltz through the opening. "Dad? Do you re- member that time that you, Mom, and me turned the basement into an opium den?"

Alan glances at Beatrix, who is concentrating on her win- dowsill. "Not really."

One turns, threading her thin wrist through the tape ring. "Yes, you do. We painted the paneling maroon? And then we bought all those beads and hung them in the door- ways? And Mom went out and got those huge throw pillows that we used instead of couches?"

Alan nods. "Sounds vaguely familiar."

"And when we were done decorating, we stayed up all night watching horror movies and smoking those candy cig- arettes. I made you watch *The Exorcist* twice, remember? That was a funny movie."

One's mother is a rather strange woman named Roxie, a woman Beatrix has no trouble believing would turn a room into an opium den at the whim of her satanic offspring. Per- haps Roxie actually used opium, or something only slightly less toxic. Perhaps she puffed suspicious substances from a long thin pipe while pregnant, and One was the result.

One is now twirling the roll around her arm. "It was when Mom still had a sense of humor, remember? Right be- fore you guys went insane and screwed up my life."

"Oh, then," says Alan. "I've blocked out everything before I went insane and screwed up your life."

Problem One gives up and drops the tape ring to the floor. "I'm thirsty. Is anyone else thirsty?"

"Now that you mention it," Beatrix says. "A diet something, whatever we have."

"Diet," says Problem One, her dark eyes sliding over Beatrix's overall-clad figure. "Dad?"

"Water would be great. I'm sweating already."

"You're always sweating already," says Problem One. She turns to the other Problem, who is using his fist to pound the tape onto the wall. "What about you?"

"Huh?"

"You want a drink or not?"

Problem Two barely glances at her. "Whatever," he says. He examines his fist, rubs it.

Problem One stares at his back, her eyes narrowing. Problem One is not used to being ignored. Beatrix wants to tell her that, though it is difficult at first, a person *can* get used to such things. A person can grow accustomed to addressing the backs of heads, a person can become inured to blank stares and aggressive silences.

Problem One leaves the room as Beatrix finishes taping and admires her own handiwork, admires how careful she has become. This admiration—for her work, for herself—must be all over her face, because out of the corner of her eye she notices that her son is smirking at her. Beatrix sees this smirk more and more; she saw it earlier that morning when Two handed her a letter from his father, the flap unsealed. She'd peeked inside, glimpsed the salutation "Dear Psycho," and quickly shoved the letter back into the envelope.

"Dad's pissed. I don't think he wants you to write any more letters to Lu," Two had said.

"It's none of your business," Beatrix replied, feeling herself flush. Yes, she had written a letter to Lu, her ex-husband's wife, but it was a perfectly appropriate letter, a *well-deserved* letter. She doesn't care what names her ex calls her. "You don't have to worry about it."

Two smirked. "I'm not worried."

And here he is, smirking again. Beatrix is so tired of it. The smirking, the mockery, the disdain. He had smirked and mocked and dismissed and disdained her until she simply could not take it anymore, until she allowed him to move in with his father and *that woman* full-time. But instead of things getting better, they had only gotten worse. The most recent problem had to do with his birthday, which he was supposed to spend with his brothers, Beatrix, Alan, and even Liv. They were going camping for the weekend. Together, as a family. But he didn't want to spend his birthday with *them,* he said. He wanted to go to some stupid baseball game with his friends. She knew she shouldn't be insulted or even surprised by this, but she couldn't help it. She had carried him for nine months. She had bathed and clothed and nurtured him. She had endured his contempt without complaint. All she asked for was one nice birthday celebration. A tidy tent. A cookout. Card games by the fire. These simple things, and he hadn't spoken a civil word to her since.

One returns with a tray of pop cans that she's slipped into foam insulation sleeves. "To keep things cold," says she, chill incarnate. Trays, foam insulation sleeves, thinks Beatrix. How can a girl who visits only a few times a month find such things when Beatrix herself isn't aware they have them?

One puts the tray on top of the coffee table—left uncovered because they plan on refinishing it anyway, whitewashing and distressing it—and grabs two of the cans. She sips from the can in her right hand and, with the can in her left, jabs Two in the ribs.

"What?" says Two.

"Take it," says One.

Two doesn't look down at the can; he is watching a spider make its way across the ceiling. "I don't want it."

"Yes, you do."

"I said, I don't."

"God, you're a shithead," says One, jabbing him again.

"Come on," says Alan. "Can't we all just get along?"

Two stares down at One, then at the can in her hand. "Knock it off."

One is unimpressed. "Take it and I will, wingnut."

Two takes the pop. One sneers at him and flounces over to the sheet-covered couch, sits, and crosses her legs. Problem Two drinks, peering at One over the can. This is not the first time that One and Two have been in each other's company, of course, but it is the first time that Two has ever looked at One in any way other than with complete indifference. Beatrix tells herself that she should be encouraged, but instead a finger of anxiety tickles her gut.

"Are you guys ready to paint?" Alan says. Alan loves to paint things. Alan has the steadiest hands in the universe.

"Sure," says Beatrix.

"Let's get it over with," says One.

"Whatever," says Two.

Twenty minutes pass in silence, until Alan disappears into the kitchen to retrieve the radio. In deference to the Problems, he tunes in to a top forty station, and rap music assaults Beatrix's ears, some woman chanting about licking someone up and down. Lick, lick, lick, lick.

"What are we listening to?" she says before she can stop herself. She is always talking too fast, stating the obvious, leaving herself open.

"It's called music," says One. She looks at Two. "I guess they didn't have this sort of thing back in the day."

"No," says Beatrix, "they didn't. They *sang* back in the day."

"That's what you call—"

"That's what I call it, yes," says Beatrix, cutting her off, letting her irritation get the best of her. "Singing. Someone plays instruments and a person actually *sings* the words. Someone with *talent.*"

One rolls her eyes and flicks her brush in Two's direction, spattering droplets all over him and the ceiling.

"Watch it," he says.

One shrugs. "I *am* watching it."

Two drains his drink and holds it out to One. "How about another?"

"You know where the fridge is. And get me one, too."

Two smiles then, actually smiles, and steps over the radio and out of the room. One paints a face onto the wall, two X's for eyes and a straight line for a mouth. As if One had just put the finishing touches on a specially commissioned fresco, Alan beams.


What Beatrix loves about Alan is that he is so hopeful. That he is able to maintain his optimism in the face of overwhelming difficulties that would defeat the most dogged. They met at a marketing seminar hosted by a company that produced vitamins and encouraged a pyramid structure of management. She could sense his profound hopefulness from across the room, saw it shining like an aura all around him. For this man, she thought, there is no mountain high enough. She would have climbed anything, anywhere, with him.

Watching him painting carefully around the windowsill, his hands so sure, she still wants to make those climbs, even though her own enthusiasm for their vitamin business waned in the early months when they hosted their own parties and tried to convince their friends to join them. Every morning, Beatrix goes to her job as a marketing director at a food company, and Alan gets up, puts on a shirt and a tie, and cheerfully makes his phone calls. And when they sit together at the end of the day, he'll recount the rude things that people have said to him, and he will chuckle into his mashed potatoes.

So how, then, does a man like him end up with a child like this one? Biology? Environment? Both? Actually, Problem One reminds Beatrix of her ex-husband, the way that she has always imagined he was as a teenager: cool, snide, selfish. She supposes what drew her to him was the belief that there was something underneath that slick exterior, something small and true that she might take into her hands, something she could feed and grow.

One has sent Two for beverages three times, twice by splattering Two with paint, once by scrawling a green line down his arm with her fingernail. Beatrix sees the weakness in her son as well, sees how he is drawn to One's hopelessness like a fish sucked into a boat propeller. One cannot fill herself up, so she will use Two if she can. That's how she is. That's how they are.

"Crap," says Alan. "We're running out of paint."

"Too bad," One says. "I guess we'll have to stop."

"No, no, keep going," says Alan. "I've got another gallon in the garage." He pauses by his daughter's side. "Thanks for the help, honey."

"Uh-huh," One says. "Remember you said you'd pay me."

"Nobody offered to pay me," says Two.

"Not my issue," says One.

Alan thinks they're funny, thinks he's a part of it. "I'll be right back!" he says, bounding out of the room.

Problem One tips her can at Two. "He'll be right back." The foam insulator slips a bit, revealing the white can, the blue and red lettering.

*Beer,* Beatrix says to herself. *They've been drinking beer this whole time. How did we miss the beer?*

Problem One glances Beatrix's way, realizes that they've been snagged. Her grin spreads across her face like syrup over a pancake, settling, soaking in. "So what?" she says. "So what?"

"I don't understand what's wrong with you," Beatrix says.

"Oh, let's see . . . um . . . *you,* maybe?" One throws the beer to the floor, where it spills, bubbling furiously, like peroxide on a wound. Two nods in approval, smirking.

This is, thought Beatrix, how much they hate her, how much they hate their own lives, what they were prepared to do about it. For a moment, she can see clearly into their collective future, watches herself monitoring the liquor bottles, coming home early one afternoon and hearing the soft laughter from her son's bedroom, the rustling of sheets, enduring the perpetual explosion her home would become.

"Slut," One says under her breath.

With a paper towel, Beatrix wipes her brush carefully, balances it atop the paint can so that it will not drip all over the floor, and slaps One smartly across the face. One opens her mouth to speak, a red rose blooming on her cheek. Beatrix takes a single step closer. "Don't," she says, warning her, warning both of them.

Maybe it's not the word or the slap or the step, but her expression—the resolve that her ex always said made her eyes flash—that silences them. In her mind, she ticks off the necessary repairs. She will cancel the birthday weekend and let her son go to his baseball game. She will send this girl back to her own mother, who will have to exorcise her child's demons as best she can. And the two of them, the Problems, will forget this single afternoon of collusion, these brief hours during which they had the same destructive agenda. Hoping for more—for family, for friendship, for a basic level of civility—is too much to ask; she sees that now. She will settle for separate but equal. Or just separate and separate. She will hold on to what little she has and be thankful that it's still hers.

Beatrix turns away and inspects the paint job, now seeing yet another thing she will have to fix. "You know what?" she says. "This green reminds me of snot."

Problem One frowns in momentary confusion before regaining her composure. She drops her hand from her cheek and tosses her hair. "Duh. That's what I told you."

Alan appears in the doorway, a gallon of Glidden's eggshell cradled in his arms. "What did she tell you?"

Looking from the Problems to her husband, Beatrix wants to start this day again, scrape it back, paint it a different shade. For him, for Alan. She bends to retrieve the beer can from the floor, pushes it firmly back into the foam sleeve. "She told me how much she likes the color."

"After all that complaining?" he says, watching Beatrix pass the can back to his oddly silent daughter. "I don't believe it."

Beatrix takes the gallon, wincing just a little as the handle bites into her fingers. "Believe it."

# BALLAD OF THE BARBIE FEET

In old photographs, they are sweet sickles, the exposed arches a pale, wrinkled surprise. Liv pores over the videos that document her childhood, watches her younger self catwalking across the suburban landscape with that perfect, tight-hipped slink, and her saucer eyes well up at the sight of what she has lost. She punches the buttons on the remote, cutting the video midstream. "This is your fault," she says to Roxie, at Roxie. "You and Dad screw up everything."

When Liv was just shy of seven, a surgeon calmed the overexcited Achilles tendons that had kept her on tiptoe since she first stood up by herself. For months after the operation, Liv walked like a person wearing swim flippers, as if the world were flat and she could drop off the edge of it at any moment. Roxie and Alan enrolled Liv in ballet lessons, not to dupe her into thinking that professional dance was a viable career choice, but to help her get acquainted with her new feet.

Nine years later, Liv's Russian ballet teachers poke at her nonexistent arches with their canes and with their fingers and frown—or worse, purse their lips in pity. "Try the jazz dance!" they suggest, averting their eyes. "How about the hip-hop?"

"The operation had nothing to do with your arches," Roxie says. "The doctors didn't touch those. It was your tendons. They were too tight."

"Your underwear's too tight. Your skull's too tight," says Liv, the kind of thing she says when her parents try to explain themselves, explain anything.

"I didn't know she seriously wanted to be a ballet dancer," Alan says. "I thought she wanted to be Mariah Carey."

"She just wants to be black," says Roxie. "No, black *and* a ballet dancer. She wants to be the world's premier black ballet dancer."

"Black," Alan says in that flat way that tells Roxie he's too tired to explore this.

They are meeting at their usual place and time: Thursday, nine P.M., in the parking lot of the library. The evening is warm and humid, and beads of sweat form at Alan's hairline. Roxie resists the urge to blot his forehead with a tissue, shifts her books from one arm to the other. She reads a lot of "women's fiction" but, lately, finds that the themes pop out at her like lame bumper stickers: *Don't date married men!*

*Don't marry gay men! Don't breed with bozos!* She has begun to taunt herself with a sweetie-pie brand of magical realism: *Mystical events concerning life and love and food preparation happen in France, in Mexico, in India, but none of them will happen here, and none of them will happen to you!*

"Liv blames us. She thinks the operation screwed up her feet and ruined her chances at ballet."

"The operation didn't do it. Nature screwed up her feet," says Alan. "God did."

Roxie snorts at the mention of God. She's studying psychology, and it brings out all her snotty agnostic tendencies, tendencies that she knows annoy Alan, not because they are dismissive so much as because they are irresolute. It took her twenty-two months of separation before she could decide on the divorce.

Alan: sweaty, cranky. "Her feet are just fine. She can still dance. Hell, she can walk, can't she? She'll get over it."

Roxie picks at her cuticles, at the nail on her middle finger that grows at an angle. Her daughter, her job, her studies, her boyfriends, and all these books with their funny-terrible sketches of dating disaster and recipes for personal ecstasy have left her feeling more irresolute than ever. What kind of magic could descend upon the homes and shops of Oak Park, Illinois? The dachshunds of peace! The egg salad of love!

Not one woman in any of those books had gone on a date at Chuck E. Cheese's, not one.

Roxie sighs. "Yes, she can walk. She can breathe and swallow, too. Maybe we should remind her of that."

•    •    •

Their split was peaceful, bloodless. Roxie kept the house, Alan the investments, and both kept Liv the best they could. At the time, Liv was infected with what Roxie called "a touch of anorexia," which meant that she was skinny and peevish and had numerous irritating tics. She'd demand an ice-cream cone and eat it with a fork, scraping the dome with the tines. The vegetarian chili was consumed one bean at a time. At restaurants, she badgered her parents into ordering mozzarella sticks and onion rings and vats of cream sauce but asked for something raw and sprouted for herself.

"I can't keep eating all these nachos just to help her get back at us," Roxie had said to her first rebound boyfriend, an Egyptian chef named Hab. "First of all, it's stupid and destructive. Second, I'm getting fat."

"Fat," said Hab, placing a hand on her ample hip. "Only in America is fat bad."

A few years later, Liv discovered that devouring truckloads of junk food in front of Roxie—she of the perpetual diet—was a far more effective and enjoyable brand of torture, especially since she could burn it all off with one good hissy fit.

"This is only my second sundae today," Liv says as she, Roxie, and Alan tour the dance supply store. "I don't know what's wrong with me. Maybe I'm coming down with something."

Roxie closes her eyes to roll them in secret. "Do you want a napkin? I like to take a napkin and wrap it around the cup so that my fingers don't get sticky."

"My fingers never get sticky," Liv says, zeroing in on some gauzy little ballet skirts that cost $75 each.

Roxie claps her hands together once, loudly, trapping them so that they cannot reach out and smack someone. "How about some jazz shoes? Miss Vronski recommended some brands for you to try." She wishes she knew a good spell to flip the sundae onto the floor.

Liv stabs at her ice cream, spraying them all with chopped peanuts. "Thanks a *lot*."

Roxie looks at Alan, whom she'd dragged along for moral support. "What? What did I say?"

"I do not need *jazz* shoes. I need new *ballet* shoes for the talent show," says Liv. "I choreographed an entire piece by myself, or did you totally forget about that?"

Roxie tries to imagine Liv as a baby, a tiny Betty Boop with tiny bowed feet. She had suffered from gas, so she smiled all the time. "Of course I didn't forget," says Roxie, "but it doesn't hurt to be prepared. I just thought—"

"Stop thinking," says Liv, licking her spoon. "You're not so great at it."

"Hey," Alan says, awake now. "Is that the way you talk to your mother?"

"It speaks!" says Liv.

"Is that the way you talk to your father?" says Roxie, grabbing for the ice cream as Liv jerks it away.


The facts: Alan had an acute midlife crisis, had an affair, and got involved with a sleaze named Mike Ritchie, Mr. Pinky Ring Pyramid Scheme with all his vitamin drinks and diet powders and voodoo. Her husband, who had spent his adult life haggling for deals and climbing the corporate lad-der, was suddenly convinced that he could make millions in a couple of short years if he harassed all his friends into becoming "distributors" and handed out flyers at the mall.

And before she knew what was happening, the crisis crept over to Roxie's side of the bed and she applied for and was accepted into the doctoral program in psychology at the state university. She took a 50 percent pay cut to work at a twenty-four-hour crisis hot line, where she did everything from counseling the suicidal to ordering the toilet paper.

And Liv? After her parents' respective crises, Liv was forced to attend her ballet school as a scholarship student, which meant that she had to swab the sweaty studios in exchange for her classes. "It's a good thing you hooked up with those suicide people," she said, "because I'm going to hang myself."

In retrospect, Roxie figures that she and Alan wanted to shoulder their burdens as gracefully as their parents and grandparents had but needed to cultivate some actual burdens first. They were tired of being comfortable; they wanted to raise the stakes. They wanted to explore—if not life and death—marital discord, mental illness, professional devastation, financial ruin, crime, and punishment. What didn't figure into the equation: There are women who still put on fresh lipstick before their husbands come home because they remember when their own daddies left for good and there was never enough to eat. Roxie had no idea that these women would have hated her.


The man on the phone is sobbing. Though Roxie has been at the hot line for close to two years, the sobbing men are still unnerving.

It seems, he says, he is getting a divorce. And it also seems, he says, that his soon-to-be ex will be taking the children to Colorado, where a river guide—complete with skinning blade and cowboy hat—will be their new daddy.

"My ex is shacking up with the Marlboro Man," he says, sobbing. "He probably hunts. He'll teach Lenore to shoot a rifle. She's only six!"

Roxie takes mental notes. For her thesis, she plans on researching the effects of divorce on the divorced and divorcing. So far, it looks as though the effects are madness, aggression, petulance, depression, weight gain, adult acne, plastic surgery, and Jerry Springer logic. Though she too has a defunct marriage under her belt, Roxie herself feels divorced from divorce. Divorcing people have sordid public affairs with best friends and neighbors. They kidnap pets, set fire to the furniture. They embark on years-long quests to humiliate each other, alienate their own children, destroy each other's property or credit rating. She and Alan simply aren't passionate enough for all that drama. It has never occurred to her to pick up a chair and heave it through the picture window or send obscene e-mails to Alan's new wife.

She wonders what it would be like to live with a man who made her feel that histrionic, that borderline. There was Hab, of course, oboe-voiced, cinnamon-skinned Hab, who had tried his best to turn her inside out, but in the end it was all so much frantic sex and food fights and a heart so sick that it required antibiotics. Now, when she thinks of throwing caution to the wind, she remembers how quickly it blows back and smacks you in the face.

Roxie listens to the man sob about Colorado and imagines pouring him some tea, tucking him into his bed, throwing an afghan over his feet. She has been trained to stay in the moment, but there are certain things she's learned. Shouldn't you share what you've learned?

"She'll hate it," she says finally.

"What?"

"Your wife. She'll hate Colorado. The Marlboro Man doesn't read books. He doesn't understand the theater. He puts ketchup on his eggs, and he coughs without covering his mouth. The cowboy hat will start to look like something else, a tumor, maybe, or a Portuguese man-o'-war."

"He's Portuguese?"

"She'll hate it," says Roxie. "Trust me."


Roxie's boyfriend of the moment is Tate, an easily distracted doctor with lashes so thick that he appears to have glued them on. After Alan, with his touchy internal thermostat, after Hab and all his hot air, Roxie has been trying men who, like camels, are good in the heat. And things had been heating up well enough to prompt a get-together with all their kids at a restaurant of Tate's selection: Café Fondue. Roxie is hopeful until she sees that Tate's daughter, Ashleigh, is stacked and sticks her chest out as if she had something to do with it, while his boy, Ryan, seems disturbed or possessed or both.

Liv fidgets with her Coke and stares at Tate. "I thought you were Egyptian."

"What?" says Tate, who had been watching his son jab at the air with his fondue fork.

"E-gyp-ti-an," Liv repeats.

Tate, somehow believing that Liv is actually interested in

his heritage, says, "I'm English and Italian. A little bit Greek, too."

Liv pokes Roxie in the arm. "What about the Egyptian guy? What's his name? Hag? Did he dump you or something?"

"We don't like Egyptians anymore," says Roxie, flipping open a menu with a flourish. "What do you guys want to eat? Do they have any breadsticks?" Out of the corner of her eye, she sees Ryan crumpling up straw wrappers and flicking them at his dad, his sister, Liv. "I always like to get breadsticks first."

"They have a nice cheese fondue," Tate says. "It's served with bread cubes. You dunk them."

Roxie is scouring the menu for some food item that doesn't involve blue flames and boiling oil when Ashleigh eyes Liv with the marrow-deep hostility known only to teenage girls. "Get her a dozen hamburgers and a cheese milkshake," she says. *"Please."*

Liv stretches, all cat, scrutinizes Ashleigh's bountiful chest. "Nice tits," she says. "How much did they cost?"

Roxie opens her mouth to add something or squash something when Ryan crosses his cuckoo-bunny eyes and dumps his Shirley Temple right into Roxie's lap.

Driving home with the drink still seeping between her thighs, Roxie thinks that Ryan's animosity, while marked, doesn't seem personal. And no one set the table on fire or had their eyes put out with a wandering—or menacing—fondue fork. She guesses she should be grateful for these things. It is amazing how much she wants to be grateful.

•   •   •

Roxie sets up for the third yard sale she's had in a year. There isn't much left to sell. Some random clocks and phones, a set of stacking tray tables, the rest of Liv's baby things, a rack of women's clothes, a couple of kitchen chairs—they need only the two—a box of rabbit's feet she found under Liv's bed. Roxie's record collection, which was spared the ax twice before, is featured prominently on the center table.

"Roxie!"

Roxie turns to see a woman standing on the sidewalk, her hand tented over her eyes to shield them from the sun. "Hi, Moira!"

"I thought that was you!" Moira marches up the driveway. This is a woman Roxie met at a bunko party, the one who set her up with Tate, the ADD doctor. "What are you doing?"

"Oh, I'm just trying to get rid of some junk. What are you doing?"

"God, *exercising,*" Moira says, her lip curling up. She gestures to the orange red tracksuit she's wearing. "Isn't it awful? Ben bought it for me for inspiration. Do I look inspirational to you?"

Moira is thin but has the kind of sallow skin that results from spending too much time indoors, skin that looks green against the red of the suit. She reminds Roxie a little of the Grinch dressed as Santa Claus, except without the potbelly. "You look great!" says Roxie.

"Liar." Moira tucks a clump of hair behind her ear. "So, can I help you bring out the rest of the stuff?"

"What stuff?"

"Stuff you're going to sell, what do you think?"

Roxie shrugs. "This is it."

"Oh," says Moira. "Okay." She unzips her suit jacket. "I hear you met my kids."

"I did?"

"Yeah. When you were out with Tate."

Roxie can feel her eyebrows fly up into her bangs. "What? Wait a minute. You mean . . ."

"Yup," Moira says. "Tate's my ex."

"Those were *your* kids? Ashleigh and Ryan?"

"I hope they behaved themselves."

Roxie unconsciously rubs the fronts of her thighs where Ryan dumped the Shirley Temple. "But . . . but you set us up!"

"Sure. You said that you were looking for a date, remember? Tate's single, you're single."

"Yeah, but . . ." Roxie trails off. She can't imagine setting up Alan with anyone she knew. It was like some sort of incest. Practically obscene.

"Tate's a tad rusty in the dad department, but no rustier than most," Moira is saying. "And anyway, one woman's trash is another woman's boyfriend. Oh, hey. That was a joke."

"A joke," says Roxie.

"What I mean is, just because he ignored me doesn't mean that he'll ignore you. We didn't click, that's all. Sometimes that's all divorce is. A fatal case of not clicking."

Roxie is about to disagree, to say: No, it's not about clicking, it's about purpose, it's about gratitude, it's about believing you're better than pyramid schemes and the husbands who are sucked in by them. But before she can speak, Moira picks up a set of plastic picnic cups. "How much for these?"

Later, Roxie's sitting in one of the chairs, watching people pick through her things, and trying not to think about
their dirty hands handling, their paws pawing, when she
sees Alan ambling into her yard. He inspects the items on
the tables—an ashtray, some measuring spoons—then sits in
the chair next to her.

"What's the deal?" he says.

"You're the salesman," Roxie says. "You tell me."

"I'll give you a thousand dollars for these spoons."

"Do I look stupid? Do I look crazy? Two thousand, and
not a penny less."

"Seriously," he says.

"I am serious. These are very important spoons. I was
going to bring them to the *Antiques Roadshow,* but they're in
Nashville this week."

Alan leans forward, elbows on his knees. "Does Liv know
you're selling her baby stuff?"

"Yes," says Roxie. "Does Beatrix know you're here?"

"Yes," says Alan. "Well, sort of. I was on my way to deliver a letter to Ward. She likes me to deliver them person-
ally."

"She wants you to deliver letters to her ex? What kind of
letters?"

Alan tips his head, looking as if he's not sure she's the
right person to whom this information should be revealed.
"That's the weird thing. They're about regular stuff. Al-
imony, visitation, vacation plans. But I don't think they're
for Ward at all. I think they're for Lu."

Roxie frowns. "Ward's wife?"

"Yeah. I think Beatrix writes these letters to drive Lu
crazy. And then she wants me to drive them over to their

house and hand them to her." He rubs his cheeks. "The plan seems to be working, too. Once, Lu answered the door with two cigarettes clamped in her mouth, one on either side, like tusks."

"How does it make you feel? Delivering these letters?"

Alan takes out a handkerchief and blots. "I hate it when you try that therapy crap on me."

"Therapy crap."

"All right. It makes me feel like an idiot. A useless idiot, if you really want to know."

"Sorry."

"Yeah. Me too." He stuffs the handkerchief back into his pocket. "So I quit the vitamin business. And I'm quitting this mailboy business. I have some interviews next week. For real jobs."

"Reality," she says, and snorts, though she likes the sound of it, the lilt of it. "I'll give you five records for two hundred bucks. That's my final offer."

Alan stays till the end of the sale and helps her clean up. She knows he does this because he is angry with his wife, but Roxie has lived apart from him long enough to find his games amusing. She offers him some leftover chicken chunks from Café Fondue as a reward.

"Why are all the cabinets open?" he says, eating the chicken standing up at the counter, scooping the chunks from the plastic bag with his fingers.

"Liv," says Roxie. "You can always tell where she's been because she won't close anything—drawers, cabinets, refrigerators, doors. She's an open book, that girl."

He tosses the plastic bag into the garbage. "When's she due home from dance?"

"A half hour. Why?"

"Let's play a joke on her."

"A *joke*? On Liv?"

"Come on." He proceeds to open every door and drawer in the place: the toaster oven, the microwave, the basement, the bathroom medicine cabinet, the drawers in Liv's bureaus. They crouch behind the island in the kitchen.

"This is ridiculous," says Roxie.

"Shhh!"

Liv flings open the back door and drops her dance bag on the floor, takes in the openings everywhere. She circles the kitchen slowly, walks around the island to see her parents crumpled there like a couple of kids. She puts her hands on her hips and squints, hard. "You guys aren't, like, sleeping together or something, are you?"

"We're not sleeping together," Alan and Roxie say in unison.

"I just don't want to know, okay?" says Liv. "I don't want to know about any of it."

Alan springs to his feet. "Let's play a game. All three of us."

Roxie looks up at him and sees that he's not perspiring at all. "What the hell's gotten into you?"

It takes some convincing, but Liv agrees to play a game that Alan digs up from the basement, a game in which someone picks a letter, then everyone has to come up with names of certain items—furniture, sports teams, foods—that begin with that letter. You get points when you think of names that no one else has thought of, but the others can vote on whether your answer is too creative.

The buzzer rings.

"Time!" shouts Alan.

"We can all hear the buzzer, Dad," Liv mutters.

"What do you guys have for 'desserts'?" he says. "I have 'nuts.'"

"That's not a dessert!" says Liv.

"Of course it is," Alan says. "Why else would people put a big bowl of nuts on the table after dinner?"

Liv shakes her head. "You are so cheating," she says. "But, whatever. I have 'Newtons.' As in Fig."

Roxie is about to blurt: But that's not the real name of the cookies, you can't split it up like that. But she keeps her mouth shut, afraid that she will ruin this fragile moment. Right now, Alan's bizarre, real-job energy is the only thing that keeps Liv sitting cross-legged on the floor, hunched over her list like a dragon around its gold. One false move from Roxie, and Liv slips back into her favorite persona: Olivia the Teenage Bitch.

"What do you have, Mom?"

Roxie purses her lips. "I wrote 'nothing' because I'm on a diet and I'm supposed to have nothing for dessert. Kind of creative, right?"

Liv shrugs, and Roxie silently gives herself a point.

"What about 'names from the Bible'?" says Liv.

"That was easy," says Alan. "'Noah.'"

"I have 'nun,'" Roxie says.

"Cute, Rox," says Alan. "Nothing, none."

"No! N-u-n. Nun. As in sister."

"Doesn't count," says Liv.

"Come on!" Roxie says, unable to keep from protesting. "I gave you Newton. You mean to tell me that there's no nuns in the Bible anywhere? There's got to be a nun!" She is sure there's a nun.

"It's not a real name. It's just a noun," says Liv, just as sure, even more sure.

"What do you have?" Alan asks her.

" 'Nebuchadnezzar,' " says Liv.

Roxie drops her pencil. *"Who?"*

" 'Nebuchadnezzar,' " says Liv. "The king in the book of Daniel who dreams about the statue with the feet of clay."

"Feet of clay," says Roxie. Alan is nodding like a horse, and she wants to kick him to make him stop it. He was the one who had insisted on the parochial schools when they still lived in the city.

"Explain it to your mother," says Alan, and Roxie does kick him. Lightly, though, just a nudge. *So he's getting a real job again, so what?*

Liv flips her list over and draws a picture of a statue. "This king dreams of a statue. It had a gold head, silver chest, brass legs, and feet of clay. Since the clay's weaker than the rest of the statue, the feet break apart, so the whole thing falls down. Daniel says the dream means that the head of gold was Nebuchadnezzar, that he was king of kings, but the kingdoms after him would get worse and worse and eventually everything would suck."

"Such a nice story," says Roxie. "Okay, what do you guys have for 'condiment'?"

But Liv isn't finished. "It's true, though, isn't it?" She points to the head on her drawing. "This is, like, say, everyone from the beginning of the world to World War One." She moves down the body, pointing to the chest. "This is people from the Depression. Here are some baby boomers.

And here's you guys," she says, pointing at the feet. "Right here."


Roxie's latest book gets right to the point: *Chocolate Is My Weakness*. The main character is a lonely woman who asks all her co-workers and potential lovers a series of questions: Would they rather stay on a Ferris wheel for two years straight or have a thumb twenty-one inches long for the rest of their lives? Would they rather have the ability to be invisible or fly? (Of course, everyone wants to be able to fly.) She marries the one guy who answers "thumb" and "invisible." At the wedding, they both fly away. At least, that's what everyone else believes.

Roxie closes the book. Here she is, a woman who has willingly dug a financial and emotional pit for herself and now reads these arch and quippy stories, these butterscotch dreamscapes, to climb out of it. What kinds of women were reading these books? More important, what kinds of women *weren't* reading these books? Moira, who looks to Roxie like the type of person who'd carry a knife in a little sheath at her ankle. No sweetie-pie magical realism for her. Or for Beatrix, Alan's wife, a great doughy goddess of a woman, all breasts and butt and temper barely restrained by her suits, the buttons threatening to spray like bullets. Even Lu, Beatrix's ex's new wife who skulks around on parent-teacher nights, Lu would open up one of the books just to crush her lipstick-stained cigarette between the pages.

Roxie reaches into her bag for the apple she's tucked there, a little depressed to have fallen back into the personal habits she's tried so hard to get free of: the endless lists, the didactic instructions, the spare piece of fruit tucked in the purse for emergencies. She has been staying later and later at the hot line, taking inventory, counting the pencils over and over and over, each time getting a different number. How is it that you learn you aren't going to be a dancer or an actress or a star? How does that slow and silent knowledge sneak up behind you and then break open over your head like some great, spoiled egg? You won't make great cookies or sew your own curtains or take a good photograph. You aren't going to beat those odds and stay married for a thousand years. What do you do when you take stock and find out that even pencils are beyond you?

Roxie takes a clean sheet of paper and one of the pencils, writes, "THINGS I AM GRATEFUL FOR," at the top of the page, then crosses it out. To hell with it, she thinks, she'll write her own damn book. It will have chapters such as "Stupid, Humiliating Affairs with Supervisors and Foreign Men," "The Pod People Who Have Replaced the Children," and "The More Things Change, the More They Stay the Same: When the New Husband Makes You Long for the Old One."

"You were right," the man says.

"Excuse me?" says Roxie. She is wearing a little paper hat, which she whips off her head before she remembers the callers can't actually see her.

"About the Marlboro Man? You were right."

"I was?" she says, recognizing the voice. "Oh! I *was.*"

"Yeah," says the man. "She was down in Colorado for three weeks and said that the whole outdoors thing got old.

The bugs were awful and everything was damp, she said. Who would have expected bugs in Colorado? And the guy was a total jerk. She wants to come back, and I guess I want her to, but I may make her wait a little."

"Well, I'm very glad for you," Roxie says. "I guess." She flattens the little paper hat. It's actually a letter from Sears, telling her that if she doesn't pay the bill, well, they may have to come over and do something intrusive and inconvenient. "Good for you," she says.

"I just wanted to say thanks," the man says. And then he adds, "Hope things are okay on your end."

"They're fine," she says. "Actually, I think Sears is going to repossess my washing machine. But, hey, other than that . . ." She trails off.

"It's always something, isn't it?"

Roxie hesitates, then sighs. "But I love my washing machine."

He has learned something, too. "I know what you mean."


Liv has been holed up in the basement for weeks, putting the final touches on her number for the school talent show. She is doing a clown theme, she says, tragic and pathetic and weird all at once. Roxie wants to weep at her choice. "Honey," she says gently, "people hate clowns. In horror movies, the clowns are always evil, okay? And even if they aren't evil, they aren't ever funny."

"Who says I'm trying to be funny? I'm a clown from another world. I'm a freak clown."

"Those are the worst kind."

"Duh. Why do you think I'm doing it?"

• • •

At the school on the evening of the talent show, parents are milling around wearing the blank expressions of farm animals, butting into the walls and one another. Roxie sees Alan and Beatrix in the hallway. Beatrix is dressed in winter white, though it's spring. Roxie absorbs the wide, schmoozy smile, imagines Beatrix dropping fishhooks into an envelope. At the sinks in the ladies' room, Roxie gets an overbright and cheerful greeting from Lu, who then dashes off without even drying her hands.

The parents are herded into the auditorium seats, and the show begins. After a few numbers, Roxie sees that, at Liv's high school, "talent" is defined as singing off-key in body glitter or wearing as little as legally possible while shaking your thang to loud, monotonous music. Roxie slides down in her seat in horror while Tate not so secretly plays games on his cell phone.

Liv is the seventeenth act. She walks out onto the stage in her silvery blue unitard and fluffy white blond wig: Smurfette gone bad. Her expression is her usual, one of intense constipation, but beneath it her neck is long and elegant, her limbs belted with tight ropes of muscle. She begins to dance, and Roxie feels her own muscles tighten first in sympathy, then in surprise, then in wonderment. All she's ever seen Liv dance were the pretty things, the sweet things, *La Bayadere, The Nutcracker.* This is rough ballet, broken ballet—it is the Tragedy of the Fallen Arches, the Ballad of the Barbie Feet—but the pain in Liv's desperate gyrations, in her powerful leaps and contortions, is real and terrible and beautiful, raw and bitter as a mouthful of Baker's chocolate.

Roxie grasps Tate's smooth, dry wrist, but in her mind it is Alan's dewy one. Look, she wants to say, to scream. *Look!* Can you believe it? Would you *ever* have believed it? She grips the wrist tighter in her hot little hand and knows that she has never seen a more brilliant performance, a more stunning debut.

# DEAR PSYCHO

August 7, 2001
To: mtractenberg@worldcom.com
Fr: WardHarrison@home.com

Mitch:

You know, I just got another stupid note from
Beatrix, first one in a while. I was going to
e-mail you some crap about marriage or divorce or
relationships, but then I realized that I was sick
of my own stories and sicker of my own half-assed
theories and dumped the message (and Beatrix's
note) in the trash. Then it occurred to me that
if *I* was sick of all this, you must be in your
death throes. Sorry, buddy. Next time the Ex has a
psychotic break, I'll try to save the bitching for
the therapist.

I just wanted to tell you one thing. The other
day, I went out and bought some gym shoes. They
were red.

Ward

• • •

*Ms. Lupe Klein and Mr. Ward Harrison*
*Cordially invite you to attend their wedding*
*Saturday, April 21st 2001*
*1:00 p.m.*
*At the Chicago Botanic Garden*
*Reception to follow immediately after the ceremony*

*Mom, this is what the invite's going to look like. Pretty cool, huh? It will also have this nice vellum overlay thingy that Annika picked out for me. And ribbons. Apparently, one __must__ have ribbons.*

*Remember, we still have to go shopping for your dress (or pants suit, or overalls, or whatever it is you want to wear). Not black, though, OK? We're trying to be festive here....*

*Love, Lu*

Posted on SPLITSVILLE.com, February 13, 2001:

Is this what normal feels like? Tired but not exhausted? Irritated but not incensed? Pleased but not ecstatic? Calm but not serene?

I guess I've reached the equilibrium I've been hoping for, right? The Ex is still an ass, but he's a tiny one. Dear Husband is, well, DEAR—so supportive and so encouraging (ha! He even stepped in and told the Ex to get off my back, and so far, so good). The boys get along with their stepmother OK but are finally starting to see that she isn't the coolest thing since flared jeans—I guess the novelty's worn off! The job's going great.

Anyway, things are good, and here I am, feeling weird about it, feeling mad about it. It's been so long, too long. You guys all said adjusting could take years, but I didn't want to believe you. I guess I *couldn't* believe you. Five years to get the courage to get out of a marriage, and then another five years to recover from getting out of a marriage? That's a quarter of my life!

God, I think I just gave myself morning sickness, and it isn't even morning, and I'm not pregnant.

Anyone else feel this way? You work so hard, go through so much, and you don't even get to be delirious with happiness at the end of it all. A lot of times you don't even get the satisfaction of seeing your Ex miserable. It doesn't seem fair, does it?

2Good2BeBlue


•     •     •

December 18, 2000
To: mtractenberg@worldcom.com
Fr: WardHarrison@home.com

Mitch:

Another fight over the boys' Christmas schedule,
but this time that asshole Alan got on the phone
to lecture me for "screwing with his wife." You'd
be proud of me, buddy, for what I didn't say,
like, he wasn't too concerned about screwing with
her when she was MY wife. But I don't want to come
to blows like we almost did a couple months ago.
Lu was so freaked out that I thought she might
call off the wedding.

Anyway, I was too tired to fight over the
schedule, so I just let them have Christmas Day,
even though it's my day. We'll celebrate Christmas
in January. Or March. Who cares?

How are things with you? Still looking for another
job?

Ward


## November 26, 2000. Instant Messaging:

BeaFREE40: Britt! We miss you (all you
guys)! What did you do for Thanksgiving?
SuuuperDawg: Not 2 much. We had pizza.
BeaFREE40: Pizza? Didn't you just have
turkey?
SuuuperDawg: We were hungry. We ate pizza.
BeaFREE40: When I called last night, Lu
sounded like she was crying.
SuuuperDawg: No she wasn't. She likes pizza.
BeaFREE40: Yes, she was. You know how you
can just tell by somebody's voice?

SuuuperDawg: No.

BeaFREE40: Come on, you know what some-body's voice sounds like when they're crying. Kind of thick?

SuuuperDawg: Huh????

BeaFREE40: What do you think she's crying about?

SuuuperDawg: No clue.

BeaFREE40: Did she and your father have a fight?

SuuuperDawg: No.

BeaFREE40. Well, all I can say is that she didn't sound happy. I told you that she wouldn't be happy.

SuuuperDawg: Whatever U say.


## Posted on SecondWivesSpeakeasy, October 23, 2000:

I'm leaving. I mean it. These people are crazy! All of them!

We're all called to a parent-teacher conference, the four of us, my soon-to-be Dear Husband (who isn't DEAR right now, or ever. I want to know why we all have to use the acronym DH on all these boards, anyway? I never would call my husband "Dear" even when he IS my actual husband, even when I don't feel like killing him).

SO, anyway, we're all there, my STBDH, the Ex, her grinning chimp husband, and me. The teacher shows us some notes that my soon-to-be stepson has been passing in class, all of them with car-toon drawings with people having sex on them.

(Totally gross, I know, but aren't all teenage boys kind of gross? It's bad, but is it that bad? I don't know! Help me!)

Anyway, the teacher flashes these nasty little drawings and the Ex starts yelling at us, accusing us of having sex in front of her kid or something (of course, the grinning chimp man is nodding sternly behind her). And then STBDH loses it, reminding them that THEY were the ones who were f*$%king around when DH was out of town, did they think stepsons didn't know what was going on in the other room? The Ex and the STBDH keep going at each other—you were the one, no, *you* were the one—the poor teacher reduced to these little lamblike bleats of pain. Then the grinning chimp stands, hitches up his jeans, and tells my STBDH to knock it off. STBDH says—can you believe this?—"Make me." Grinning chimp says maybe they ought to handle this situation like men. I'm thinking, what do you mean, *handle this like men*? What do men do in situations like this? Box? Arm wrestle? Duel at first light? Good thing that some other teachers heard the shouting and broke the whole thing up, otherwise, who knows what would have happened?

I have to say, I'm in shock. I can see the headline now: PARENT-TEACHER CONFERENCE SCANDAL: MEN ARGUE ABOUT WHO CAN PEE THE FARTHEST. I cannot believe the soap opera my life has become.

I have to get out of here.

LaVidaLoco

• • •

September 15, 2000
Beatrix Reynolds
N. New England Avenue
Chicago, IL

Dear Psycho:

    a.  Stop the useless threats
    b.  Get your head out of the gutter
    c.  Book a therapy appointment
    d.  Get a prescription

Ward

P.S. Here's a check for $43.19 for school supplies.


September 10, 2000
Ward Harrison
W. Cortland Avenue
Chicago, IL

Ward:

    a.  The boys have come back to my house from yours
       repeatedly without having taken a bath or shower. You
       need to pay more attention to their personal hygiene
       while they're at your house.
    b.  I have repeatedly bought Ollie new outfits that promptly
       disappear every time he visits you. He returns to mine
       wearing ripped clothing he's outgrown. I want the boys
       returned to my house wearing the clothes I bought them.
       I won't keep replacing clothing you're responsible for.

c. *Britt told me that he attended one of those park dances on Saturday. Do you know what goes on at these dances? The kids practically have sex on the dance floor! I find it highly disturbing that you'd be so irresponsible as to send our twelve-year-old to one of these dances just so that you and Lu can go out to dinner.*

d. *Britt and Devin have informed me that you and Lu have "made out" in front of them. I wonder if you understand how suggestible the children are at this age, and how vulnerable. Highly sexualized behavior that occurs at these dances you're sending them to or at your home in front of them can confuse and overwhelm young boys, causing all kinds of problems.*

*You wanted to be a custodial parent, Ward. If you want to KEEP being one, I suggest you get your act together.*

*I'm still waiting for the check for your portion of the school supplies: $52.14.*

*Beatrix*

August 30, 2000
Alan Reynolds
N. New England Avenue
Chicago, IL

Alan:

I think you're under the mistaken impression that you have a role here. You don't. There are decisions that Beatrix and I must make, discussions we must have, as the parents of our children. Advise Beatrix all you want on your own time, but I have nothing to say to you. I'm not impressed by the bullshit macho posturing.

Ward


August 25, 2000
Ward Harrison
W. Cortland Avenue
Chicago, IL

Ward:

I'm going to have to step in here and put an end to this insane letter writing. You're upsetting my wife and my household, and I won't tolerate it.

In the future, please direct all communications to me. (And you can be a man and pick up the phone.)

Sincerely,

Alan Reynolds


August 9, 2000
Beatrix Reynolds
N. New England Avenue
Chicago, IL

Beatrix:

First things first: Don't send my wife any more of your nutball letters. After you bit her head off for buying the kids some CDs, well, let's just say she isn't interested in

being your pen pal. Or your lackey. The next time Ollie
forgets his gym shoes, you can get off your ass and drive
over here to get them. Lu's not a delivery person.

Second, Lu didn't encourage any of the kids to call her
"Mom," that's why they call her Loopy. If you want
them to stop calling her these "pet names," YOU can
tell them how insecure you are.

Third. I had no say about the man you brought into my
sons' lives, and you have no say about the woman I
brought into my life. Suck it up.

Ward


*July 15, 2000*
*Ms. Lupe Klein*
*W. Cortland Avenue*
*Chicago, IL*

*Dear Ms. Klein:*

*I think that it's time to establish some ground rules regarding
my sons and your role in their lives. I understand that you've
been encouraging them to call you "Mom," and when they
wouldn't, you asked that they use some sort of silly pet name. I
am their mother, you are their new stepmother—these are
very different roles. It is your job to treat my children civilly
and with respect, the same way you might treat a niece or
nephew of whom you are fond. It is MY job to parent them. Do
not expect that they will love you just because their father
does. Do not expect that you will be "filling in" for me while
they're at your house; you are not qualified to make important
decisions regarding their care. For example, Britt is NOT
allowed to get his ear pierced. You have caused me much grief*

because you promised that he could get it done on his next birthday, and I had to be the one to disappoint him. You need to discuss these issues with me before making any promises.

I'm not trying to be difficult, I just want you to put yourself in my shoes—I don't know you, yet I have to trust you with my children. Your respecting my position as their mother would go a long way in building that trust.

I hope we have an understanding.

Sincerely,

Beatrix Reynolds

P.S. The pants you bought Devin were totally inappropriate for school, and I returned them. Enclosed you'll find a check for the purchase price.

Posted on SecondWivesSpeakeasy.com, March 19, 2000:

Hi, all. I'm new here—not a second wife yet but will be next year!—and have been reading a lot of the postings with great interest. I have a question for all you longtime second wives: When did you stop being afraid of the first wife? My significant other's ex looks like the Michelin Man, if the Michelin Man was packing.

Also, when do you stop wondering why the first wife left your SO (well, aside from the fact that

she must have brain damage)? Ms. Michelin's second husband stands around grinning all the time,
like a chimp with gas. What's that about?

LaVidaLoco


December 14, 1999
To: mtractenberg@worldcom.com
Fr: WardHarrison@home.com

You won't believe this crap. Or maybe you will.

It's my year to have the boys for Christmas Eve,
so we planned on taking her to my parents' for
dinner and then Lu's parents for dessert and
coffee and a couple of gifts. (On Christmas
morning, we have the boys till ten.) But when I
tried to confirm the plans with Beatrix she pulls
her Mrs. Hyde routine. She demands the boys for
dinner on Christmas Eve and then wants to have
them back on Christmas Day at 8:30 am so that
they can all drive to Alan's parents downstate. I
said no way, it's my day and the plans are set.
So of course the psychobitch gets to work on the
kids, especially Britt, telling him how hurt her
mom and dad will be if they don't see their
grandsons on Christmas Eve, how bad Alan's parents
will feel, how the world will explode and baby
animals will die and Humpty-Dumpty will never be
put back together again. Poor Britt then begs me
to change the plans because his mom will be angry.
I called the bitch up and screamed at her to keep
our boys out of it, and all she would say was:
"This is what the boys want to do. Ask them."

I hate that woman. I cannot imagine why I ever
married her. Tell me, why did I marry her?

Ward


•   •   •

Posted on SPLITSVILLE.com, September 25, 1999:

So I knew this would happen, but I'm still not happy about it. The bimbo finally moved in. They haven't even known each other that long, they're not even engaged yet, but they move in together. I just think it's so irresponsible, but when I said that to my mom, she said, "Well, YOU moved in with Alan." Come on! It's so different! I've known Alan for years! We were engaged! I didn't pick up some bimbo off the street!

And you know what really bugs me? I'm knocking my-self out, working full-time and then driving this kid to soccer practice, that kid to the dentist, and taking it and taking it from my oldest, who's decided to become a mouthy teenager all at once, and my ex and his bimbo are waltzing around without a care in the world, with no responsibility for any of it. HE's the one who fought for the joint custody! So why isn't HE taking the kids to the dentist? Why is HE allowed all these weekend getaways?

I saw the bimbo at my son's soccer game, cheering like SHE was the mother or something, and she didn't even say anything to me. Not one thing. And neither did my ex. Is it stupid of me to want a little acknowledgment? A little respect? These are MY children that she'll be spending time with. You'd think they'd understand how important it is to discuss how much this stranger will be in-

volved in my children's life. The ground rules.
There ought to be ground rules, don't you think?

2good2BeBlue


June 12, 1999

Dear Mom and Dad:
Please stop putting notes in my backpack.
It freaks me out.
Love, Devin


June 10, 1999

Beatrix:
Waiting for something that will never come
will only make you more insane than you already are.
Ward


*June 8, 1999*

*Ward:*
*I'm still waiting for a check for $38.25 for your por-
tion of the other bathing suit and the camp towels.*
*Beatrix*


• • •

June 2, 1999

Beatrix:

Let me get this straight. Because some neighbor dog bit your cat's tail, I have to buy you new towels? Are you crazy?

Wait, don't answer that.

And as far as my not understanding how much it costs to raise a child, let me remind you that the boys live with me 170 days out of the year (26 weekends a year plus 104 week days plus 14 days of vacation). That's only 25 days less than they live with you.

Here's a check for one of the bathing suits.

Ward

May 17, 1999

Ward:

I don't think you appreciate the incidental costs involved with clothing, housing, and generally raising a child. (Remember, you're not responsible for keeping the boys as many days as I am.) Just the other day, when Devin was supposed to be watching the neighbor's dog, he accidentally let him into our house. That dog chased Little Bit all over the house and bit her on the tail. I had to rush her to the vet to get stitches, and it cost more than $200.

I included the bathing suits and the towels on the camp list because Devin is required to wear blue bathing suits at camp (he told me you bought red and orange) and needs special towels to take back and forth. As you may not realize, wet towels crumpled up in a camp bag may get mildew, and I don't think household towels are appropriate for this purpose. I'd appreciate a check for the remaining $68.24.

Thanks,
Beatrix

May 9, 1999

Beatrix:

Enclosed you will find a check for $558.96 (65% of $859.95). I just bought the kids a couple of bathing suits myself and am not required to pay for the suits that you chose to buy him to wear at your house. I have no idea why you'd include the purchase of two towels on this list.

Ward

May 3, 1999

Ward:

I signed Devin up for day camp and paid the following fees:

Registration: $25.00
8 weeks tuition: $800.00
Uniform: $34.95
Two bathing suits: $59.98

*Two large towels: $45.00*
*Total: $964.93*
   *As per our agreement, your portion of this bill is*
*$627.20 (65% of $964.93). I'd appreciate your paying*
*this bill immediately; the last time you were late, and*
*I had to pay interest charges on my Visa.*

*Beatrix*

Posted on theothermother.com, April 14, 1999:

Hi everyone:

I'm not a stepmom or even close to it, but I am
dating a man with three young sons. I have to say,
you guys are scaring me! Some of you have all
these horror stories! My boyfriend's kids are always nice to me. Am I just lucky, or is this the
calm before the storm?

Lulu34

February 18, 1999, Instant Messaging:

   BeaFREE40: So, did you guys do anything fun
over the weekend?
   SuuuperDawg: We went to the park, but it
was 2 cold, so we went home. And then we went
to Lu's party. She let us toast marshmellows
in her fireplace.
   BeaFREE: MarshMALLOWS. With an "A." And
who the heck is LU?

•    •    •

November 7, 1998

Beatrix:
I'll be out of town from Monday to Wednes-
day. You can call my cell if there's an emergency.
Ward

October 2, 1998

Beatrix:
I'll be out of town this weekend, so I'll be unable to watch the boys as you'd asked. I did call
my mother and she said she'd be happy to baby-
sit, if you have a need.
Ward

September 12, 1998

Beatrix:
I'll be out of town for the next few days. In an
emergency, I can be reached on my cell. You have
the number.
Ward

•    •    •

August 15, 1998

Beatrix:

I'll be out of town next week, so I was wondering if you were available to watch the boys Thursday and Friday. Please let me know.

Ward

June 7, 1998. Chat Room Transcript:

BeaFREE40: He's so jealous. You should see his face when he comes to get the boys. It's sad, really, if you think about it. I almost feel bad for him.

Beasmom: I feel bad for him.

BeaFREE40: I said *almost*.

Beasmom: Bea, honey, can you just call me on the phone? I know you bought me this computer and set everything up, but typing on this thing makes my joints ache.

May 29, 1998
To: mtractenberg@worldcom.com
Fr: WardHarrison@home.com

Mitch:

I met someone. And I'm starting to think it could be going somewhere.

I'm freaking terrified.

Ward

•    •    •

May 4, 1998

Beatrix:

When you say that you don't know what's more important than your plans, you mean you don't understand what's more important than YOU.

Forget it, it doesn't matter. I'll be around that evening.

Ward

*May 1, 1998*

*Ward:*

*Frankly, I don't understand what's more important than this. Can't you just move your plans to another date?*

*Beatrix*

April 28, 1998

Beatrix:

The plans are fine, except for the bit about Sunday. You'll drop them off between 5 and 10? Can you narrow that down a bit? I had plans for that night. . . .

Ward

•   •   •

*April 15, 1998*

*Ward:*

*The wedding is planned for Saturday the 23rd—I enclosed a copy of the invitation so that you have the details. As the boys are an integral part of the ceremony, I would like to have them from Friday evening for the rehearsal dinner through Sunday evening, when we leave for our honeymoon. We'll drop them off at your house sometime between 5 pm and 10. We'll be in Paris for ten days, returning on the 5th. I'll pick the boys up from school on the 8th.*

*Please confirm these schedule changes with me at your earliest convenience.*

*Beatrix*

March 15, 1998
To: akstone@earthlink.net
Fr: luklein@goldrealty.com

Hey, Annie,

Remember that blind date I told you about? The one with that dad guy? The one I was absolutely dreading? Yeah, um, well . . . wasn't as bad as I thought. Actually, it was good. More than good. Even with the tucking the shirt in thing that all dads do. (Is this some sort of dad rule? Tucking AND belts?) Anyway, he's smart and funny, with curly hair, great hands. Talented hands, if you know what I mean. Talented everything. I know we nice girls aren't supposed to sample the wares before the third date, but I couldn't help myself.

Geez, I hope he calls me, cause otherwise I'm going to feel like the proverbial ho. (Uh, is that a proverb????)

Lu

•   •   •

February 16, 1998

Beatrix:

This is the third time I've requested that you file the quit claim deed on the house. I'd rather not go through the lawyer about this, but if it's not filed by next month, I'll have to.

Ward


January 4, 1998
To: mtractenberg@worldcom.com
Fr: WardHarrison@home.com

Mitch:

It's D-Day. My own personal D-Day. I almost can't believe it. I'm a single man.

Things had been going pretty smoothly for a while. No fights, none of her stupid ass notes, no fighting me every time I come to pick up the boys. I even shook hands with that guy she's shacked up with. (The boys seem to think he's OK, so that's something.) I was nervous to see Beatrix in court. She looked good, lost a little weight, the works. But as we were going through it, as the judge decided this and that, I realized something important. I loved her, I totally loved her, but I never really liked her. She's picky, she's literal, she's demanding, she loves to get on her high horse and ride the thing till he's dead. I don't want to be with that kind of person. The kind of person who, if you fell off your bike and broke your leg, would yell at you for riding irresponsibly instead of asking if you were OK.

And while I was having these thoughts, I noticed something else. Her shoes. She wore these red shoes that I bought for her way back when we were dating, these "mary-janes" she always loved. I think it was a slam, you know? I think she was trying to tell me that she could kick up her heels without me.

So I know you'll say that I'm reading too much into the whole thing, but I don't think I am. I think that's it. And now it's over. Done. Dead.

I wish I knew what to feel.

Ward

Gratitude Journal:

*September 12, 1997*

*Devin, trying so hard to be a man. He shakes Alan's hand.*

*Britt, the boy you can take anywhere, the boy who will help with anything. Just this morning he made me pancakes (or tried to. He forgot the eggs, the batter burned solid, and we had to throw out the pan).*

*Ollie, sweet Ollie. He says "good morning!" to the squirrels in the yard, he wants to be a vet and a juggler and a police person. He actually said "police person." Who couldn't love a boy like that?*

*Alan, who showed me what real love and support is. I finally have a fully committed partner to share*

*my life with. I can't describe the feeling. I'm dizzy,*
*I'm flying. (Ha! I'm relieved!)*

*Friends who give me unconditional love no matter*
*what's happening with me or what size I am.*

*I've lost 14 pounds!!!!!*

August 20, 1997
To: mtractenberg@worldcom.com
Fr: WardHarrison@home.com

I've been thinking about this unconditional love
concept, and you know, I've decided that it's
bullshit. The only people you love unconditionally
are your kids, and even that isn't always as true
as we all pretend it is. Could you say that you'd
still love your wife in the same way if you
discovered she was an embezzler? If she gained 200
pounds slamming Twinkies? If she started sleeping
with some guy she works with? Is it realistic to
think that we'll love another person no matter
what they do? Is it realistic to plan our lives
as if nothing will ever change?

## July 18, 1997. Chat Room Transcript:

BeaFREE40: I don't know why he can't see
how hard this is for the boys. I don't care
what the court says. He's a bastard.
Beasmom: He is their father.
BeaFREE40: But he's still a bastard.
Beasmom: This is upsetting you. Let's chat
about something else. Get it, chat? I'm getting pretty good at this high-tech stuff,
don't you think?

BeaFREE40: What else is there to talk about, Mom? This is my life, you know. My life.

Beasmom: Yes, honey. But this is what you wanted, isn't it?

BeaFREE40: So it's my fault? I'm getting what I deserve?

Beasmom: I didn't say that.

BeaFREE40: You didn't have to. I can see it in people's faces. They have no idea the pain I had to go through living with that man. They think I'm some sort of floozy.

Beasmom: Honey, nobody uses the word "floozy" anymore.


June 19, 1997
Beatrix Harrison
N. New England Avenue
Chicago, IL

Dear Ms. Harrison:

As per the custody order dated May 5, 1997, your sons, Devin, Britt, and Oliver Harrison are to spend Thursday and Friday of every week and every other weekend with their father, Ward Harrison. If you continue to interfere with this court-ordered custody arrangement, or attempt to deny Mr. Harrison his right to see his sons, we will have no choice but to pursue legal avenues to rectify the situation.

If you have any questions, feel free to contact me at this office.

Dana Sherry,
Esquire

• • •

*February 7, 1997*

*Ward:*

*What the hell are you trying to pull? Having our sons jumping back and forth from house to house with their underwear in a paper bag doesn't benefit THEM, it benefits YOU. They're just little kids! Have you thought of how difficult this will be for them? Why can't you accept that they're happy with me, in one place? Why can't you see that this is the best thing for them? Are you trying to get back at me? Well, let me tell you right now that it won't work. It's low, Ward, low even for you, to use our sons like this. And I'll tell you something else: I'll fight you every step of the way.*

*Beatrix*

February 2, 1997

Beatrix:

I agree that the boys need a father, which is why I've decided that weekend visitation isn't enough. I have no interest in being some sort of Disneyland dad with no real relationship with his children. I've investigated joint physical custody and believe this type of arrangement will suit the boys best. My lawyer and I are working on a proposal. As soon as we have the details hammered out, I'll let you know.

Ward

• • •

January 2, 1997
To: mtractenberg@worldcom.com
Fr: WardHarrison@home.com

I picked the boys up the other day and they told
me that the asshole has moved in with them. Can
you believe this? It's been what, four months!?

I'm trying to pull it together. I have to pull it
together. I swore in front of the kids. I've never
done that before, but some shithead cut me off and
I called him a fat fucking fuck—that's exactly
what I said. Ollie looked so shocked, I thought he
was going to pass out. He must think I've lost my
mind. Now I'm worried that he'll tell his crazy
mother and she'll sue me for having a potty mouth.

How could she move in with that guy so soon?

Ward


December 13, 1996

Beatrix:

I wonder sometimes if you have any idea how
ridiculous you sound. If the boys aren't supposed
to be involved in "adult matters," then why did
you introduce them to your boyfriend before we
even separated? Why were the boys attending
Alan's family functions before I even knew the
man existed? And why would you tell them that
you were "just friends" when it was clear to them
and to the rest of the world what you were
doing?

You are in no position to moralize. If they're confused and upset, maybe YOU need to look into the mirror for the reason why.

Ward

December 4, 1996

Ward:

As per our temporary agreement, I will be picking the boys up from school so that we can spend my birthday together. Since we are planning a late dinner, I will need to keep them overnight. Please let me know if there's any problem with this.

I'd also like to bring something else to your attention. You need to be more careful about what you say to the boys. Frankly, I don't care what you think of me, but please don't take your anger out on our children. They're scared and confused enough as it is. They need their father right now, not some babbling lunatic. I don't know what you told them about Alan, but I don't appreciate your comments or insinuations. They don't understand adult matters and shouldn't be involved in any of them. As I've told you repeatedly, the breakup of our marriage has nothing to do with him and everything to do with YOU. If you're looking for a villain, you might try looking in the mirror.

Beatrix

• • •

Posted on SPLITSVILLE.com, November 28, 1996:

```
What  a  great  website!  I'm  so  glad  I  found  you
guys.  I'll  start  hunting  down  those  receipts  right
away.  I  had  another  quick  question  for  you  all:
I  received  a  small  (2K)  incentive  bonus  from  my
employer.  Is  this  considered  income?  I  got  it
after  we  separated.  Thanks!


2Good2BeBlue
```

### November 2, 1996

Beatrix:

Hey, thanks for turning off the boiler and opening all the windows when you left. The autumn leaves on the dining room table were an especially nice touch.

Ward

Note on kitchen table:

*November 1, 1996*
*Good-bye!! Good luck!! Feel free to take the lamp in the living room. I've always hated the damn thing.*

·     ·     ·

*September 10, 1996*

*Ward:*
*I don't think you understand. Nothing in my life is*
*up to you, now.*
                                        *Beatrix*

September 6, 1996

Beatrix:
Do whatever you have to do. But I don't want
that sweaty asshole you're hooked up with to
step foot in my home.
                                        Ward

*September 5, 1996*

*Ward:*
*I'll be moving out on the first of the month. I'd ap-*
*preciate it if you'd make arrangements to be away*
*from the house during the hours of 8 am to 4 pm. I*
*don't think we need to make this any harder than it*
*has to be.*
                                        *Beatrix*

•    •    •

August 9, 1996
To: mtractenberg@worldcom.com
Fr: WardHarrison@home.com

So maybe you're right, it's just like back in high
school, all chicks are bitches and we just have to
deal with it. I just wanted to know when she
stopped wanting to be married to me. How long this
has been a sham, you know? I thought that was a
pretty simple question. I mean, we're talking
about the woman who has an answer for everything.
So why doesn't she have an answer for the most
important thing? (Yeah, I know, maybe she doesn't
think it's the most important thing. Shut up
already.)

You won't believe this book she gave me,
supposedly written by some marriage expert. She's
an expert all right. She's been married four
fucking times, I looked it up. What the hell am I
supposed to do with a marriage book by some dumb
bitch who's been married four fucking times?

Shit. Everything's shit. And my language is going
down the fucking toilet.

Ward


July 20, 1996


Beatrix:
I don't believe you. But I guess it doesn't matter now.

Ward

•    •    •

*July 19, 1996*

Ward:

*I got your letter and I don't know what to say except that I'm sorry. I have tried, tried as hard as I could for as long as I could, tried to tell you I wasn't happy, tried to get you to understand, but I can't try anymore. I just can't.*

*It's clear to me now that we're not meant to be together. You're a good man and a wonderful father, but we've both changed so much. It goes deeper than the arguments we've had about having another baby, or my job, or your job, or who's doing what around the house—I just don't love you in the same way, and I'm not sure if I ever did. We were so young, we never got a chance to experience the world—what did we know about love and marriage and all of it? Now we—and that means the both of us—will have a chance to find out. In the long run, I know this is the right thing. If you looked into your heart, you'd know it, too.*

*I'm giving you this book, which has really helped me to understand what went wrong with us, and what we can do to keep that from happening with other people. I hope it helps you, too.*

*There is something you need to understand: Alan has nothing to do with my decision. I've known for a long time that I had to leave, meeting him simply gave me the courage to do it. I never meant to get involved, I never meant to hurt you or the boys. Believe me, this has caused me more anguish than you'll ever know.*

*Beatrix*

July 17, 1996

Beatrix:

I've tried to write this letter so many times in so many different ways that I'm hip deep in wadded papers. I think I just have to come out and say it: I don't know what went wrong.

I try to see it, understand it, but I can't. I guess I didn't meet your needs. I worked too hard. I didn't help around the house or help with the boys enough. I didn't listen. I didn't encourage you enough, or in the right way. I pushed you into the arms of someone else. I don't like cats. Is that it? I don't know.

But whatever it is, I'm sorry for it all. For disappointing you, for taking you for granted. Right now I have no clue what would make me turn my back on you the way I must have, what small shiny thing could have captured my attention for so long that you felt I had forgotten about you. Because I didn't. I never have.

Do you remember that day we were window-shopping, just a few months after we met? You were so busy staring at those shoes you liked— they were the red ones, you always liked red, red like your hair—and you walked right into a telephone pole, nearly knocking yourself out? And you laughed so hard that you were snorting, and you demanded to know why I wasn't snorting, too? Why I kept asking you if you were hurt rather than collapsing into hysterics myself? And you assumed that I was just a nice, concerned guy hoping that you didn't have a concussion? I wasn't a nice guy then, I'm not one now, as you've said many times. So, I'll tell you, I asked if it hurt because standing there, watching you laugh, I hoped so much that I could knock you out like that, I wanted it so much my heart hurt. I wanted you to feel that same way. I wanted you to hurt, too.

So, I can see that this isn't making much sense, but then, my head's a fucking mess; I feel like I've just plowed into a telephone pole, only it isn't funny. I don't think I can get through this, and I don't want to. Do you want to? Do you really? I'll say I love you, but after ten years of marriage, it's not that simple. I everything you. You're the mother of my children. There isn't a corner of my world that doesn't have you in it, somewhere, in some way.

This guy you've been with, I won't forget about him, I can't, but I won't ask about him, either, I swear—I don't want to know. He's your memory, your secret to keep. I want you—laughing you, snorting you, you in the red shoes. And I know that we can work it out if we tried.

Let's. Please. Try.

Ward

# SAFEKEEPING

In an old photo album, dragged out only on holidays, there is a picture of Lu on Santa Claus's knee. With lips pressed into a grim smile, one eyebrow cocked, and her arms folded tightly across her chest as if to protect her heart, Lu looks every inch the kindergartner who turned her back on Santa Claus a long time before, dismissed him the same way she dismissed all those other Technicolor phantoms of childhood: the Tooth Fairy, the Easter Bunny, the white rabbit on the cereal boxes. *Silly rabbit.* This photograph was a sentimental favorite of Lu's mother's. It was taken around the time she had divorced Lu's father. "If I'd wanted another child to raise," she'd told Lu, referring to Lu's dad, "I would have gotten knocked up again."

Lu thought of this photograph when, on the way to the mall, she and her three boyfriends saw Santa Claus. Santa was driving an old Dodge Dart striped with blue house paint and talking on his cell phone. A cigarette that bobbed from the corner of his mouth threatened to set his frothy beard on fire. Lu, who had just given up cigarettes for good for the fifth time in her life, could practically taste the tobacco.

"Hey," said Britt, the middle boyfriend. "Santa."

"What? Where?" yelled Ollie, the youngest, craning his neck to see. "That's not the real Santa. Santa doesn't smoke, does he, Lu?" Just the other day, Ollie told her that she was not allowed to have a baby for at least five more years, when he was fifteen. "I'm the baby of the family," he'd said. "Me."

"Looks like Santa's a smoking fiend," Britt said.

"No, he isn't."

"Duh," said Britt, an expression that always sent Ollie into a spasm of flailing limbs aimed in his brother's general direction and which did so now.

"Guys," Lu said halfheartedly. "I'd like to get to the mall without having to make a pit stop at the emergency room, okay?"

"Ow!" said Ollie. "He hit me!"

"No, he hit me," Britt said.

"A likely story," said Lu. "If you keep it up, I'm going to drive this car into a ditch."

"Is that any way to speak to your stepsons?" said Britt.

"It's the only way to speak to your stepsons," Lu said.

"I don't know why we have to go fricking Christmas shopping," Britt mumbled irritably. "It's not for weeks and weeks."

"I don't want what happened last year to happen again," Lu said.

Ollie stopped flailing. "What happened last year?"

Last year, Lu had decided to blow her holiday budget on a weekend getaway for Ward, plus a little joke gift she claimed was from Picky the cat. It was the first year that they had all three boys on Christmas morning, yet she hadn't thought to remind them to get anything for their father, nor had she bought presents on their behalf, as her own mother used to do. It simply hadn't occurred to her until they were gathered around the tree, when she saw that she and the boys each were tearing through piles of gifts, and Ward, poor Ward, was left holding nothing but a picture of a lakeside cabin in Wisconsin and a spiked dog collar.

At the time, the boys hadn't noticed. And here, Ollie didn't even remember.

"Your father didn't get any presents last year, that's what happened," said Lu. "Not one of you bought your own father a present."

"I was only nine last year," Ollie said.

"And I don't have a car," Britt added.

Lu glanced at Devin, the third and oldest boyfriend, sitting in the front passenger seat, but Devin wasn't in the mood to provide excuses. Actually, Devin wasn't often in the mood to provide much of anything but scowls, sneers, and vacant stares that made him look like a photograph of himself rather than the real thing. The approaching holidays had made him touchier than ever, and she had begun to dread coming home. He'd scrape his flinty eyes over Lu, over Ward, and over his own brothers and then whip his head away as if he couldn't bear the sight of any of them. "At least he's quiet," Lu had told Annika, her sister. "At least he's not taking drugs or robbing little old ladies."

Annika had said, "How do you know what he's doing in his spare time?"

Devin turned up the volume on his Walkman and jerked his head spastically. He loved music, but music did not love him back. "I gots ta go," he muttered.

"Yes, you do," Britt said, sending Ollie into a theatrical giggling fit.

"Yoodoo!" said Ollie, stressing both syllables, yoodoo, yoodoo, reminding Lu of the vast amounts of spam she got. She had spam on the brain. She read all of it that wormed through her filter, mostly because of the names. Spam was never from Sally Smith or John Jones. Spam came instead from the mailbox of Yes Yoodoo. Tragically Pigged. Transport P. Intoxicating. The names tickled her brain like poetry. They seemed to provide a running commentary on her life, a sly sort of jabberwocky. Just that morning, she'd gotten a message that read:

```
You look familiar. Haven't we met somewhere
previously?
Fathers, do not exasperate your children. Instead,
bring them up in the training and instruction of
the Lord. [Ephesians 6:4]
Lu Klein, are you searching to shop for
antidepressants?
Adults are obsolete kids.
Gray hairs are signs of wisdom if you hold your
tongue. Speak and they are but hairs, as in the
young.
To accept civilization as it is means accepting
decay.
```

There was something about it, that message, something nonsensical yet apt. And then there was its mystery sender,

Disagreeably Dimorphosed. Now that she thought about it, Lu thought it was as good a label as any. And this was what she said out loud: "I'm Disagreeably Dimorphosed. Capital D, capital D."

"Huh?" said Ollie.

But Lu could see Britt nodding in the rearview mirror. "Maybe you're just plain disagreeable, no capital?"

"I don't know. Perhaps I'm less Disagreeably Dimorphosed than Tragically Pigged," Lu said.

Britt snapped gum he wasn't supposed to be chewing on account of the retainers. "Could be."

As they passed, Britt waved at Santa, and Santa waved back cheerily, ash spraying out the window like seed.


Lu turned the car into the parking lot, shut down the engine, and herded the boys into the mall. True, it was early in the season, but the crowds, the relentless holiday Muzak, and the dispirited plastic wreaths with their limp red ribbons made Lu's head ache even before the shopping began.

In front of a cart at which a bored teenager sold clip-on ponytails, Lu turned to her recalcitrant crew. "Where to?"

The boys looked at her like a trio of cats, as if to say, *This is your show, Mrs. Claus. We're just along for the ride.*

"Okay," said Lu. "How about we try the Gap first?"

"My favorite store!" Britt said with excessive sarcasm.

"Your father likes the Gap," Lu said in a prim voice that embarrassed her as soon as she heard it. Being with the boys sometimes made her that way, prim and fussy, though she tried not to be. They were skilled at eliciting defenses, getting backs up. And the more they saw it happening, saw that you were on some downward spiral toward schoolmarm, the more they enjoyed themselves.

In the store, Lu started flipping quickly through sweaters. "What do you think of these, guys?"

Ollie climbed into the center of the circular rack and stuck his head up in the middle. "I'm a Christmas tree!" he said.

"You're a Christmas fruitcake," Britt told him. "Those sweaters are nasty, Lu." Devin drifted over to stacks of oversize jeans, bobbing his head arrhythmically.

"Okay," Lu said. "No sweaters." She turned to the next rack, where desperately wrinkled dress shirts crumpled in on themselves as if they were ashamed. "How about some of these?"

Britt flipped his retainer out of his mouth and sucked it back in. "Doesn't Dad have like sixty of those?"

"A hundred!" Ollie said, popping like a jack-in-the-box from the center of the rack.

"I don't think Dad needs a salmon-colored shirt, Loop," said Britt.

Ollie crawled out from under the rack. "Salmon is a fish!"

"He does have a lot of shirts," said Lu. "I don't know. We need something. *You* need to get him something."

"Give us a break," Britt said. "We just got here."

That's when Lu saw the man, hovering behind the boys. Because he was wearing khaki pants paired with one of the nasty Gap sweaters, Lu guessed that he was an employee or manager who didn't appreciate the public denigration of the merchandise. But then he pulled little yellow cards from his pocket.

"This is for you," he said, handing them each a card, which they took without thinking. "Have a nice day."

"What's this?" said Britt, but the man was already walking away, the bald spot on the back of his head gleaming under the fluorescent lights.

Lu looked down at the yellow card: "God holds you in His hand and in His heart." Next to the message was a smiley face.

Ollie frowned at the card, his lips moving as he read. "I know this already," he said. "Does the man think I don't know this already?"

Devin sneered, tossing the card to the ground. "*I* don't know this," he said, his voice thick as a smoker's. "Who says God cares about us?"

Ollie bit his lip, and Lu could see he was calculating the benefits of a tantrum. "Ignore your brother, Ollie," she said.

"Right," Devin said in a flat voice. "Ignore me."

Was Devin seething or sarcastic or his characteristic nothing? It was so hard to tell. "Devin's just mad because I won't buy him one of these pretty sweaters," said Lu. "But we're here to buy presents for your dad."

"*Christmas* presents," said Ollie. He glared at Lu and then at Devin. "I'm keeping my card."

"Sure you are," Devin said. Britt yawned.

"That's fine, Ollie. Do you need me to hold it for you? I can put it in my purse."

"No," Ollie said. "I'm going to hold it in my hand. Just like God holds me in His."

• • •

Next stop, Old Navy. More sweaters, cargo pants with pockets ballooning off them like polyps, kitschy old-man pajamas, mango-and-banana-colored shirts that Ward would never wear. Pink shirts were "in" back when Lu was in college, where Lu had majored in bad boyfriends. The first, a blue-eyed blond, tan as a surfer, often wore pink shirts to accentuate his coloring. It made him look innocent, he claimed. He'd told her this while lying naked on her dorm room floor, waggling his penis at her.

"I'm not sure if pink is right for your dad," Lu said.

Britt poked at the tables of clothes and racks of garments. "All this stuff sucks."

"What are you talking about?" said Devin. "You have tons of crap from this store."

"I'm talking about Dad. He can't wear any of this."

Ollie tugged on Lu's arm. "Devin said 'crap.'"

"Stop saying 'crap,' Devin."

"Well, when you put it that way . . . ," Britt said, snickering.

"Are we at your house on Christmas or are we at Mommy's?" Ollie said.

"Mommy's," Lu told him. "You'll be with Daddy and me on Christmas Eve."

"I thought we were going to be at Grandma's on Christmas Eve?" Britt said.

"Early in the day you will. But you'll be at our house for dinner. Then you go to Mom's Christmas morning, and then I think it's Aunt Louise's afterward," Lu said, surprised that she could keep it all straight. Blended family holidays were less blended than they were pieced up and fractured, balled up like old drugstore receipts at the bottom of a purse. With

Lu's mom and dad living in two separate states and Lu in a third, with Ward's sons alternating households on alternating Thanksgivings, Christmases, and Easters, Lu and Ward ran from one end of the country to the other, one house to the next. The gifts piled up, and the kids couldn't even remember which grandparent or stepgrandparent or not-really-my-aunt-but-whatever did the giving. Sometimes Lu herself gave up entirely and got on a plane to visit her own family by herself. On those occasions, it was hard not to feel a shameful relief.

She checked her watch, figuring that she had less than an hour before the boys' patience would be worn down to the nibs and she would be stuck buying all the presents alone. And of course that would be the easier thing. But after her colossal gaffe last year, she wanted this year to be authentic. She wanted each of Ward's sons to say to him, "I picked that out for you myself, Dad. Do you like it?" Just one genuine Christmas, and she would be satisfied that she had done her job right.

"Let's move on," she said. "There's a Carson's a couple of doors down. Maybe we can find something there."

Carson's, unfortunately, had some sort of thing for T-shirts with "funny" sayings on them. The boys, unfortunately, also had a thing for T-shirts with "funny" sayings.

"Look at this, Lu!" Ollie said, holding up a bright orange T-shirt. *I'm a Secret Agent!* shrieked the shirt. *This is my disguise!*

"That's cute, Ollie."

"Can I buy it for Daddy?"

"Uh, why don't you look through some of the other shirts?"

*Beam me up, Scotty. Denial is cheaper than therapy. I'm with Stupid.* All the reasons why beer was better than women and why women were better than men. There was *Sorry, this is not a slogan,* but in letters so tiny that you had to have the shirt three inches away to read it. Britt took a liking to *Mad as a box of frogs* and got about as mad as a box of frogs when Ollie didn't understand what it was supposed to mean.

"*Huh?*" Ollie said in that irritating way of his, curling his lips up to the gumline.

The huhs alone could drive a person crazy, Lu thought. Rule number 4,289 of stepparenting: Beware the huhs! "Ollie, don't needle your brother."

"But I still don't know why the frogs are mad," Ollie said.

Britt shrugged. "How about this, Ollie?" he said, holding up a shirt: *This is my clone.*

Ollie frowned. "Ooo!" he said, getting it, grabbing at it.

A woman motoring her way through racks of wrinkle-resistant slacks, blabbing into her cell phone, smacked into Lu and didn't stop to apologize. "Ham?" the woman shouted into the phone. "Since when do you like *ham?*" Lu rubbed her shoulder. When she was young, she used to think that people were full of delicious and dangerous secrets, private thoughts about desire and despair. Now she knew that mostly they thought about meat products and who was getting the milk.

"That would make a great shirt, don't you think?" said Britt, reading Lu's thoughts. "*Since when do you like ham?*"

"That's stupid," said Devin, oddly angry. "That doesn't mean anything."

"What about my shirt!" Ollie yelled, forgetting to whimper.

Lu took the T-shirt gently from Ollie's hands. "This is a good shirt, but I'm sure we can find something better in another store, don't you think?"

"When?" Ollie demanded. "When will we find something?"

"Soon," Lu soothed. "We'll find something soon."

Lu put the shirt on the rack with all the others, hoping to make a quick escape, when Devin said, "There's that guy again."

They all turned and saw the man from the Gap, handing out his little yellow cards. "What's he doing, following us?"

"I'm sure he isn't," Lu said. "I'm sure he's just going store to store or something."

"He's coming this way," Britt muttered. "He's probably going to quiz us on God or something. Get ready, Ollie."

"I'm ready," said Ollie.

The man marched in their direction, high-stepping like a majorette. His eyeglasses were huge square affairs that took up nearly half of his face. The strap of his canvas bag cut into his soft belly. "Here," he said, and dealt Britt, Ollie, and Lu a yellow card.

"But you already gave us these," Britt said.

The man smiled, a mirror image of his card, and turned to Devin.

"I don't want that," Devin said. The man smiled even wider and tucked the card into Devin's shirt pocket.

"Get your hands off me!" Devin yelped, but the man was already moving on, his canvas bag parting the sea of shirts. Lu marveled at the man's audacity. Nobody touched Devin. Nobody gave him stuff he didn't want. Nobody gave him stuff he *did* want. Once, Lu had bought him expensive boots he'd been begging for after watching him slog through the snow in his Converse sneakers, after listening to him complain about his frozen feet. A month later, in a box in the laundry room, she found the boots, lacy with cobwebs.

"Is that guy crazy?" said Britt.

"Now I've got one card for each hand," Ollie said.

"*You're* crazy." Devin yanked the card from his pocket and ripped it in half. The two pieces fluttered from his hands like moths.

"Why did you do that?" Ollie said. "Lu, he ripped the man's card."

"But he didn't rip yours, so everything's okay, right?" Lu could tell that Ollie wasn't buying her logic, but he chose not to protest. That was a miracle in and of itself.

Devin was glaring at the man's back as the man stalked off into the lingerie section, handing his card off to two unsuspecting old ladies buying Tummy Tamers. "If that guy comes near me again, if he freaking touches me again . . . ," he said, trailing off.

"Relax, Dev," Britt said. "Here. I found a shirt for you." *Heck is for people who don't believe in gosh.* Devin yanked the shirt off the hanger and threw it across the men's department.

"All right, that's enough!" said Lu. "What's gotten into you guys?"

Devin didn't bother to respond, retreating into his usual fog of people-be-gone. Ollie continued to beg for the *This is my clone* T-shirt, making Lu's gums ache with irritation. Britt merely smiled and held up one last shirt, one with a line she recognized instantly from the movie *Jaws: I think you're going to need a bigger boat.*

•   •   •

Lu led her boyfriends from Carson's and out into the mall, moving swiftly toward the bookstore. Surely there was something there that the boys could get Ward. A Dilbert calendar, the latest business book that Ward would never open, a crossword puzzle collection. A sign at the entrance of the store screamed AUTHOR SIGNING TODAY! but no names were mentioned. Lu thought it was pretty funny.

"Look," she said. "Anonymous author signings!"

"So?" said Ollie.

"What the hell are we doing here?" Britt said.

"Loopy! Britt said 'hell'!" Ollie blared.

"And so did you," Britt said.

Lu sighed. "Can we stay focused, please?" she said. "Think: Gifts for Dad, gifts for Dad, gifts for Dad. It's your purpose, your mantra. It is the central idea around which your life revolves."

This attempt at humor got another "Huh?" from Ollie and a blank stare from Devin. Britt, however, laughed. Britt the Fork-Tongued, Britt the Berserker, the "problem" child—the one who had gotten himself suspended from school as well as every sports team he joined—had recently become her favorite. And it wasn't because she recognized herself in him, because she didn't. As a girl, she had been more like Devin, hard and numb and unforgiving, dragging around her resentment like a club foot. Compared with that, Britt was sort of a macho drama queen: histrionic yet brash, a teen Tarzan. You had to admire him for it.

She watched as Britt scanned the stacks of best sellers, declaring them lame, more lame, and totally lame (not necessarily in that order). If she had been more like him as a child, a fighter, she thought, what kind of person would she be now? If she'd told her own stepmother, hand on hips, "You're not the boss of me!" If she'd thrown a fit every time her mother tried to paint a wall or rearrange the furniture. If she had demanded from her father extravagant gifts and even more extravagant vacations but kept insisting that no one loved her enough. Perhaps if she had done all her fighting when she was young, she would have a better handle on things now.

Then again, maybe not. Maybe Britt wasn't any more prepared for his future than she'd been for hers, for this strange job she had. Stepmother. She'd looked it up and found that the word came from some term meaning "to step in," back in the days when regular old mothers dropped off every two minutes from consumption or exhaustion and other women had to step up to replace them, but Lu thought that it really meant something else. A step *down.* A step removed. A place where the children looked at you and you looked at them and all of you could see way too much.

Speaking about seeing too much, the pink and orange and black words screamed all around her—*How to F&\*% Like a Porn Star, How to Stay Fit Forever, Investing for Idiots*—and she had to wonder if the bookstore people put this stuff out just to make all the customers look stupid. And what was with all the management books? *The Three-Minute Manager, Managing for the New Millennium.* Who was doing all this managing, and so very badly? She remembered that Mr. Pink Shirt told her that he'd been accepted to a management program after college. She kept asking, "But what will you be managing?" mostly because he didn't know the answer and it made him furious.

Lu felt the vibration of her cell phone in her purse and dug around to find it. Here was another problem: these stupid phones making everyone so available to the universe, so beholden to it. She hated that the world could find her, wherever, whenever, that they knew she was like all the rest of them, filled with random thoughts about lunch meats and logistics. There were no secrets anymore. No privacy. No dignity. Every moment was a "funny" T-shirt.

"Hello?" she said, sure it was the Lowickis, clients who disliked every single one of a dozen homes she'd shown them but who still called her every fourteen seconds for an update.

"Hello, Lu. This is Beatrix. Is Devin with you?"

Lu flinched, trying to understand why Ward's ex was calling on her cell phone when Devin's was perfectly functional. She wondered if this was going to become a habit.

"Lu?"

"Yes," Lu said. She felt a familiar churning in her gut, the one she got whenever she had to talk to Beatrix. She once met a woman, a second wife, who hadn't been acknowledged by her husband's ex in a decade. Lu knew which of the two situations was *supposed* to be preferable, but . . .

"Lu, can I talk to Devin, please? It's urgent."

"Oh! Yeah!" Lu said. "Just a second." Urgent? What was urgent? Was someone dead? Maimed? Psychologically unglued?

She found Devin leafing through an issue of *Maxim*. "Devin? Your mom's on the phone."

Devin rolled his eyes and took the phone. "Yeah?" There was some chatter from Beatrix on the other end, and Devin replied, "No, I can't." More chatter, louder, pleading. "I just can't." Chatter, sharp and angry. "Because I can't." Finally, he pushed the END button on the phone and handed it back to Lu.

"What's up?" Lu asked.

"Nothing," Devin said. "She wanted me to come for dinner. She's making burgers. She knows I don't eat red meat."

*That* was urgent? Lu wanted to say. *Burgers?* Instead she said, "Oh well. You guys can go to dinner if you want. She'll make you something else."

"We're shopping for Dad."

Peeved, Lu dropped the phone back into her purse. "I know. I mean, I was the one who talked you into coming. But you could have explained that to her instead of just saying, 'I can't.' I'm sure she would have appreciated a reason."

"I didn't want to explain. And I don't care what she'd appreciate." His face hardened. "Why do you always defend her?"

Lu had the urge to burble an Ollie-like "Huh?" "I'm not defending anyone."

"You're doing it right now."

"I'm just saying—"

"Right," Devin said, rolling the *Maxim* into a tube and smacking one palm with it. "Are we done with this store yet?"

She felt her body stiffen involuntarily. "In a few minutes. Keep looking."

Lu left Devin at the magazine rack and pretended to browse among the business books. She told herself that, to him, it must feel as if every adult in the world had gone mad, divorcing, changing jobs, moving, marrying strangers with weird extended families with whom Devin would be expected to make nice. Because of such things, some kids got middle-aged and exasperated before their time, bitching about their parents like soccer moms about their children. Others, like Devin, held on to their resentments, nursing them like orphaned kittens until the resentments seemed to take on their own lives, walked around on needle-sharp claws. Her own experience taught her all this, but it hadn't taught how horrible it would feel to be on the other side. To be caring for someone else's kid and have that kid turn around and lump you in with all the other people who have pissed him off or let him down.

She idly picked up a copy of *Who Moved My Cheese?* from the top of an enormous stack. The book, a parable about cheese and mice, was supposed to teach readers how to "manage change" in work and in life. Manage change! How in the hell do you do that? Lu looked around wildly for someone to share her disgust, someone other than a disgruntled teenager. Some grown-up person. A frosty-haired woman in stretch jeans stood next to her, flipping through a picture book written by someone famous, Billy Crystal or Tom Brokaw or Boris Yeltsin. "How is a book about cheese supposed to help a person manage change?" Lu said to her.

The woman took a baby step backward. "I heard that book was good."

"Good for what?"

She was rattled by Lu's questions; the woman's head shook like Katharine Hepburn's. "My brother read it. He liked it."

Lu scoffed. "Marry a divorced guy with kids, then talk to

me about managing change." She added a smile, hoping to show the woman she was kidding, but the woman sidled away, slipping into the travel section. *Great,* thought Lu, *I can't manage my cheese, and I'm scaring all the nice people.*

She put the book back on the stack. She might not be much of a fighter, but she wasn't as fatalistic as she used to be, not really. Hadn't she traded in all those bad boyfriends for a new set, for Ward and his sons? Before she was aggressively passive, now she was passively aggressive. There was, she told herself, a huge difference between the two.

"Loopy," Britt said, "I'm not finding anything."

"I found these," Ollie said hopefully, holding up some comics.

Lu looked over the comics. "And I guess those are for Dad?"

"Well . . . ," Ollie said. "He could read them first."

"Nice try," Lu told him. "Let's take a look in the back of the store. If nobody sees anything, we'll go somewhere else."

Lu and the boys poked through the histories and the biographies with little luck and no consensus. She was just about to suggest that they move on to Bath & Body Works for rosemary-honeysuckle shaving gel when they stumbled onto the author signing, tucked into a dark corner. A girl, no more than twenty-two or -three, sat at a table piled high with books and not one customer. Over a blue bra, the girl wore a tank top that read, *Hot Young Writer,* something that might have been cute if she hadn't been so hot and so young and if her eyes didn't have the guarded, slightly contemptuous look of the terrified. Lu felt a jolt of sympathy for the girl. Maybe she had majored in bad boyfriends, too. Maybe someone had moved her cheese.

No such compassion from the boys. A sneer buckled Devin's lips. "She's not hot."

"Who's not hot?" Ollie said.

"Shhh!" said Lu. "She'll hear you."

"She isn't so young, either," Devin added.

"What do you mean?" said Lu. "Of course she's young!"

Britt patted her arm in the way he did when he thought she needed to have the world explained to her yet again. "Look, Loop. *Mad as a box of frogs* is one thing. But you can't just go around wearing a shirt like that, okay?"

"But—"

Now Britt's voice was gentle, pitying. "Even if you wanted her book, you couldn't buy it. You just couldn't."

Out in the mall, the recycled air smelled like Pine-Sol and cloves and feet. They hadn't bought a single gift; all they had to show for their trip were a few smiley-faced God cards and an issue of *Maxim.* Lu had no idea where to go next, what to try.

"Puppies!" Ollie said, shouting.

*"Huh?"* said Britt, just to annoy her.

In the midst of the Christmas chaos, the local Humane Society had set up some sort of pet fair. There were stacks of cages with dogs and cats and rabbits up for adoption, volunteers in matching shirts. Ollie begged to go look at the "doggies," and Lu relented; they could all use a bit of puppy love.

Britt marched up toward the cages. "Who's the bitch?" he

said loudly. When people turned to stare, he pointed at a Welsh corgi mix. "What? I meant the dog."

Ollie tugged on her sleeve. "Loopy, Britt said—"

"I know what he said, Ollie. Let's pretend we don't know Britt and look at all the doggies and kitties, 'k?"

"Doggies," said Devin. "Geez."

Lu couldn't bear to see the cats—she had a thing for cats, she would have taken every single one of them, including the rabid and the feral. They focused on the dogs instead; she was sure she could resist the dogs. They petted an old black Lab, an overweight beagle, and a mutt with three legs. "He gets around just great!" a volunteer said as the three-legged dog skipped around the floor.

"What about the Welsh corgi?" Lu said, peering into the cage. "She's cute."

"Let's get it!" said Ollie. "Let's call it Corgi!"

" 'I'm with Stupid,' " Britt said.

"You're just mad because Corgi likes me better."

Lu looked at the dog, and the dog stared back solemnly. Probably not a purebred, but corgi enough. Corgi-ish. And not jumping around or panting or licking, which Lu liked. She herself wasn't neat, but she appreciated neatness.

"Lu?"

Lu turned to the dark-haired woman who stood next to her, recognizing her as the mother of one of Ollie's schoolmates. But what was her name? Something with a G. Something good-witchy, like Glinda. Oh, yeah. "Hey, Glynn."

Glynn—who must have introduced herself to Lu on half a dozen occasions while they waited for their respective kids in the school yard and had to endure Lu's willful amnesia every time—seemed shocked to find Lu had finally remembered her name.

"Yes!" she said as if praising a troubled student. "Glynn!"

She sounded so enthusiastic that Lu said, "Yes! Hi!"

"I thought that was you. I recognized you from the school yard. And," she added, "from the parent-teacher conferences."

"Right," said Lu, face burning. At one particularly memorable parent-teacher conference, Ward and Beatrix's husband, Alan, had had a shouting match that nearly led to blows. Lu had stood there, unable to move, almost breaking out in hysterical laughter as she noticed the hand-drawn poster that framed the men's battle: "My Words to Live By," the poster said. "Verbs, because they DO something!"

But Lu had heard in the school yard that Glynn was divorced and remarried herself, so maybe she had suffered her own soap opera moments. Maybe her new husband and her old husband brawled regularly at parent-teacher conferences; maybe, these days, interspousal brawling was all the rage.

"These are my stepsons, Ollie, Britt, and that's Devin."

Glynn smiled at Ollie. "Are you getting a dog for Christmas?"

The enthusiasm was catching. "Yes!" said Ollie.

"No," Lu said. "We're just taking a break from shopping right now. What are you looking for?"

Glynn pointed to a boy who jumped up and down in front of the dog cages, outpuppying the puppies. "I promised my son, Joey, a pet."

"Why don't you take that one?" Lu said, pointing to the corgi.

"I'm really not a dog person," Glynn said. "We were looking for something smaller."

"Oh," Lu said, strangely disappointed. "How about a cat?"

"Um, smaller. I was hoping that they'd have a guinea pig. Or maybe a hamster."

"What good is a hamster?" said Devin, oblivious to Lu's warning glare.

"Well," Glynn said lamely. "They're cute. And they run around in those little plastic balls."

"And that's supposed to be fun?" Devin said, practically shouting. "What do you do, kick it around?"

"Devin!" said Lu. "What's the matter with you?"

Devin turned away and turned up the volume on his Walkman, his whole body saying: *Whatever.*

"Sorry," Lu said to Glynn. "I don't know what his problem is. Normally, you can't even get him to speak."

"It's all right, I understand. The boys always want dogs. I don't know why. An unconditional love thing?"

"Yeah, maybe." Lu scrutinized Devin for signs of implosion or explosion, but the moment seemed to be over; he was busy mumbling to the music and tapping the bars of the corgi's cage. The volunteer unlocked the cage, and the dog stepped out gingerly. It didn't look like the sort of dog that offered unconditional love. It looked as if it were gauging the belly rub, table food, and master bed potential of each passerby. It was scanning the crowd for just the right sucker. *Come here, sucker!*

Devin murmured softly, secretly, to the corgi, ruffling the dog's ears in a gentle way at odds with his stiff back and his permanent hostility. Behind him, Glynn observed them with a weird expression on her face, as if they were pitiful and a little depressing, but vaguely so, like news reports from distant countries. Lu didn't think that was quite fair. Periodic brawls aside, they weren't doing so badly, were they? Other families, regular families, didn't look so stable, either.

Flashing Glynn an overbright, positive grin, Lu stuck her finger out and the corgi gave it a brief, velvet sniff.

"Loopy?" said a plaintive voice. "Can we go see Santa now?"

Lu estimated that the Santa line was about forty miles long, give or take a dozen.

"Why the hell did you promise to let him do this?" Britt said as they inched up another few steps. "Are you trying to kill us all?"

"That's how I bribed him to come shopping," Lu explained impatiently. "Just like I promised you a video game and Devin a CD."

"Can't me and Dev go get some ice cream or something?"

"I want you to see me with Santa!" Ollie yelled.

"This is gonna take forever," Britt said. "Times like these, I wish I had a gun."

A gray-haired man standing in front of them gave Britt a look, but Britt stared back boldly. "Yes? Can I do something for you? Do you need assistance? Shall I fetch an elf?"

"Shut up, Britt," Lu said. "Sorry," she added in the man's general direction, but she didn't really mean it, and the man could tell.

"You should teach your children better manners," the man said gruffly.

"Yeah, okay," Lu said. "I'll get right on that."

"We're not her children," Ollie added helpfully.

"She's our wicked stepmother," Britt said.

"That's wicked *Nazi* stepmother to you," Lu told him, enjoying the incredulous look on the gray-haired man's face as she said it.

She rubbed her forehead, but the pain—induced by repeated renditions of "Holly Jolly Christmas"—wouldn't abate. It was clear this trip was a bust; she'd barely survive the line, let alone get back to shopping for Ward. She would just have to come back here another day and pick up some shirts or some ties, wrap them, and put the boys' names on them. Maybe that's what she should have done in the first place. Why drag everyone out here just so that you can say you did? Lu thought that too many people lived their entire lives that way. People who insist they are doing things for others, when they are simply doing for themselves, so that they can tell everyone that they did the right thing. Someone once commented that Lu's sister, Annika, was sacrificing a lot to bring her triplets to term. Her sister, hugely pregnant, looked down at her own belly in amazement and said, "You think I'm doing it for them? I don't even *know* any of these people!"

Sighing, Lu stood on tiptoe to see Santa put another little kid on his knee—not because she was all that interested or that sentimental, but rather to convince the boys that there was action up ahead. "Do you think it's the guy we saw talking on his cell phone on the way here? Smokestack Santa?"

she wondered aloud, not really caring that the boys ignored her. She remembered back to the last time she herself sat on Santa's lap, the time immortalized in her mother's favorite photograph. Her mother had insisted on going to the department store, though Lu hadn't wanted to go. Lu's father was supposed to pick her up; he'd promised to take her to the movies. Lu's mother, however, knew some things that Lu had not: the fact that he had taken up with a receptionist named Winnifred and the fact that Winnifred didn't much care for other women's children.

"How much longer till Santa, Loopy?" Ollie whined in his best "I'm still a very tiny boy" voice.

"A couple of weeks, you loser," said Britt.

"I'm not a loser."

"Speaking of losers, here's our friend again."

Making his way down the line, God Man doled out his yellow smiley-faced cards to the line-weary parents and grandparents. Next to Lu, Devin tensed.

"They're just cards," Lu murmured. "No big deal."

"He better not touch me," said Devin.

Ollie opened his mouth, but Lu shushed him before he could begin. "Devin, relax. It's okay."

"No, it's not okay. It's not."

In front of them, the gray-haired man was taking a yellow card. "Merry Christmas," he said. God Man didn't respond. He took a card from his stack and held it out to Devin.

Devin smacked the card to the ground. "Keep that shit away from me."

"Hey!" said someone behind them. "Watch your mouth! There are little kids here."

"Look, sir," Lu said, "we've already got a few of your cards."

God Man looked at the card on the ground and then at Devin. He took another card from his stack. "I think this is something you need."

Devin smacked this one to the ground, too. "I said, get away!"

"God loves you," said the man.

"No, He doesn't," Devin said. His voice had taken on a strange, squeaky quality, as if someone had a hand around his throat.

"Hey!" Lu said. "Are you listening to me?"

"He does love you," the man insisted as if he hadn't heard.

"He *doesn't*," said Devin.

"He feels your pain. He holds you in His heart."

"He doesn't, He does *not*!" Devin shouted, the veins in his temples standing out.

Tentatively, Lu put her hand on Devin's arm, and he shook her off, but not before she felt his muscles trembling. "You need to go," she told God Man as firmly as she could. "Now."

"You are a beautiful child of God, and He loves you."

Devin's shoulders collapsed inward. "You don't know," he said. "You don't know anything about anything." And then, suddenly, horrifyingly, he let out a sob, right there in the middle of the mall. Tears squeezed out from the corners of his eyes.

Britt looked about as freaked out as Lu had ever seen him, and Ollie cowered against her leg. God Man reached out to touch Devin, but Lu stepped between them. In the reflection of his glasses, her own furious face stared back at her. "Leave."

"God loves him."

"We heard you the first time. And the second and third and eightieth."

"God loves all the sinners in this world."

"That's right," said Lu. "I bet He loves you, too, even though you have no clue when to give it a rest."

The man's mouth opened, a wan little O, the yellow card poised in his hand. "I just want the boy to know."

Lu poked a stiff finger in the man's soft chest, daring him to try to touch Devin again. "And I want you to get the hell away from us." Her limbs felt light and strong and fast. She thought for a second that she could break this guy's nose with one good cuff, God Man or not.

The man stared at Lu for a moment, astonished. Then he stuffed his yellow cards into his bag and stomped off, not bothering with the rest of the line.

Lu swung around to Devin, who swiped at his face with a clawed hand. She wanted to ask him what was wrong, but she could see the anguish in his face, could see that it was huge and real but also shapeless and unnameable. He didn't know the answer, and she knew that asking the question would just make it worse. All around them, the Santa line was still and quiet, waiting for what came next. From across the mall, a dog howled, lending a mournful note to "Jingle Bells."

Lu started at the sound. "I just thought of the perfect thing to get Dad," she said, surprising herself. Ollie and Britt looked at her expectantly, but Lu stayed focused on Devin. "Well? What do you think?"

Devin blinked his reddened lids, looking her in the eye for the first time in weeks. "Yeah," he said. "Yeah, that's good."

"Okay," Lu said. "Let's go."

The three of them left the Santa line for the Humane Society, Ollie silent for once, as if he actually understood what was going on. Lu didn't say anything, either, but she did allow herself one small gift: As they walked, she dug around in her purse until she came up with a single tissue, crumpled but clean. Devin didn't need it, his tears had dried, but he said, "That's okay," and she said, "Keep it anyway," and for once, he did.

# PICTURE OF HEALTH

By the time Moira returned with the groceries, Ryan and I were in a state: *Such a state they were in, you wouldn't believe!* First was the kiwi that I had innocently peeled instead of sliced, which sent him into a thirty-eight-minute screaming jag, complete with limbs flailing Gregor Samsa style. Then there was the Super Ninja mask he had to wear but could not locate in his closet or under his bed, which he had probably worn to his father's house, which I refused, on principle, to drive over and fetch for him. And there was, as usual, that tone, the "why doth my God try me with imbeciles" tone—coupled with the chubby little arms akimbo—he used whenever he wasn't getting his way, now, immediately, that brought me as close as I would ever come to homicidal.

The tone was because I made the most egregious of all errors; I threw away half an Oreo that he was—didn't I get it?

was I *stupid?*—saving to feed the lightning bug he'd caught in the yard the night before, a bug that had perished from fright or by choice almost the moment he was thrust, winking weakly, into a jelly jar.

His mother had told him that the bug was sleeping. The Oreo was to be its breakfast.

"Moira, what was I supposed to do? He took a swing at me."

"So you, brilliant thing that you are, decided to take one at him? What the hell's that supposed to teach him?"

Moira and I had been married for nearly two years, though we had been living together for almost four, along with her two children, Ashleigh, fifteen, and Ryan, seven. These twenty-two months had become increasingly more violent, or rather, put increasingly more violent thoughts in my head. I had never hit a child before Ryan, never thought I, with my high boiling point, my twelve years as a fifth-grade teacher, could be pushed even to raise my voice, let alone pushed past words. This was just the beginning of the things you learn about parenting someone else's children. They teach you not about what you are, but about what you are not.

"I think it's going to teach him not to hit me again," I said moronically, because I knew before Moira even opened her mouth that if Ryan didn't hit me again, it was only because I had reminded him that I was bigger than him. "It was just a swat on the butt. Just one. And then I sent him to his room."

"He says that you dragged him to his room," Moira said.

"I picked him up and put him there, yes. There was no dragging. I didn't drag him. I don't know why he says those kinds of things." Moira was looking out onto the porch that I had demolished three weeks ago with the intent to rebuild, her back to me.

"He's having a hard time with his father being around so much all of sudden," she said. "It confuses him, so he acts out with you. You know. A man he can trust? Why can't you just give him a break?"

I said then what I always said. "He already gets too many breaks. There has to be a limit." I knew that in an hour or two, when Ryan told me that I was really his favorite, his *daddy* daddy, I would feel like a monster.

Moira whipped around, glared. "Look. *Look.* Just don't hit him again, okay?" she said, and so that I understood the conversation was over, she began to empty the organically grown fruit into the sink, throwing it hard enough to put fresh bruises on the peaches in addition to the organic ones.

"Hey," I said. "What did the peaches ever do to you?"

Ashleigh burst in through the back door, hair freshly purple from the dye job she convinced us she deserved after earning a B in her summer English course.

"Hey, Mom. Hey, Ben," Ashleigh said. "Want to see what I bought? It's so cool." She reached into a bag and pulled out a filmy white thing with some sort of lace or webbing hanging off it. I couldn't even imagine what it was for. Or I didn't want to.

"What is it?" asked Moira.

"It's a *shirt,* Mom, what do you think?"

"I have no idea. What goes under it?"

"Under it? *I* go under it," said Ashleigh.

"Uh-huh," said Moira. "You and a camisole."

Though I was sure this was exactly what Ashleigh expected, even wanted, to hear, she said, "Mom! You don't wear anything under this! It's *supposed* to be sheer, hello!"

"You're fifteen, hello. You wear camisoles."

"I don't even own a cami-whatever."

"Borrow one of mine."

"I *can't* borrow yours, Mom," Ashleigh said, then added something I believed she had been itching to say to her mother for months, the reason she'd bought the filmy unwearable thing in the first place. "I have bigger *breasts* than you, you know."

Moira poked her index fingers into the sides of a paper grocery bag, and it collapsed obediently. "I'll buy you a camisole. Or how about an undershirt? Barbie, like you used to wear."

"You're just jealous," said Ashleigh. "You are. Men stare at me all the time."

"Your boobs are hanging out. People stare. The same thing would happen if I forgot to put on my pants."

"I don't think so."

When Moira and I were still just dating and emanating pheromones others claimed hung about us like a fog, Ashleigh and I were often mistaken for father and daughter, that's how close we were. I taught her to play softball, to pitch, to catch, to slide and steal. I taught her how to ride her bike again after a minor scrape with an out-of-control in-line skater years before had her too frightened even to sit on the seat. I taught her how to make tomato sauce, peach pie, and s'mores. Her doctor father started coming to ball games and piano recitals out of jealousy, an emotion he hadn't shown a glimmer of when he came upon Moira and me making love in the backseat of her car while parked in the lot of his office, Moira's idea. (She's wicked, but not that wicked. She thought he'd already gone home.) But his paternal attention waxed and waned like the moon, and Ashleigh was mine. Was.

Then Ashleigh's body popped like a kernel of corn, and she started wearing tops so small that her breasts burst from the neckline and sides. You could see her marveling at her own cleavage, smiling, sometimes drawing her elbows together at the dinner table to darken that dark furrow, drag us all in.

If it wasn't obvious, Ashleigh wasn't convinced it was actually there. She thought others wouldn't see, or else they would forget from one day to the next.

I stuck my hand in the crisper, sifting through the vegetables for the least battered carrot. "Hey, doc," I said through a mouthful, like Bugs Bunny, "you ain't allowed to have boobs until you're thirty-five."

I got some stiff smiles, nothing more. "Boobs!" said Moira. "Look how you have us all talking. Ashleigh, why don't you go and get ready for Auntie Flo's?"

"Can Devin come with us?"

"No, Devin can't come with us."

"Why not? I haven't seen him since—"

"Yesterday," I said. "Oh, Devin!" I gasped, clutching the half-eaten carrot to my breast. "Oh, Devin!"

Ashleigh sniffed, was annoyed with the teasing. This, like her breasts spilling from her tops in a deliberate imitation of romance novel cover art, was new. "Yesterday was the first time I saw him in ten days because we were in stupid Florida," she said, "remember?"

I felt a sinking in my gut, a feeling I was getting used to. "I thought you liked *stupid* Florida."

"Yeah, well, not for ten whole days! Anyway, why can't I ask Devin to come with us?"

"Your uncle is very ill. This is a family visit," said Moira.

"Well, Devin is almost like—"

"Don't even go there, Ashleigh," Moira said. "I don't have anything against Devin, but your boyfriend of three and a half minutes does not qualify as family."

"You're being mean."

Moira sucked her breath in sharply through her nose, the way she did when she was trying to keep herself from saying horrible, terrible, cruel things, things that, if I read the look on her face correctly, she thought you deserved to hear. She had been sucking her breath through her nose a lot since her favorite uncle was diagnosed with cancer and since he had refused to get treatment for it.

"Your uncle is ill. This is not about you, do you understand?"

"All right, all right, I hear you!"

"No, you don't. But it doesn't matter. Get ready to go."

Ashleigh's narrowed eyes wished many gruesome deaths upon her mother, but Moira, unfortunately for Ashleigh, didn't even catch head colds. I watched Ashleigh ram the "shirt" into the tiny silver bag in which it had been delivered to her, probably by some slatternly store clerk with black lipstick and a secret pierced labia, and added my two cents' worth.

"And don't even *think* of wearing that."

•   •   •

I fell in love with the children first, a wriggling toddler in a grocery cart, an exhausted ten-year-old clutching a red purse.

I had offered to go to the store for my mother to spare her the ordeal of shopping with my father, who had suffered a series of strokes. I gathered Macintosh apples—my father's favorite—in a bag, all the while sneaking looks at the cart parked by the potatoes.

"Sit down, Ryan." The girl tugged on the boy's fat baby arm when he tried to stand in his seat. "Mom's gonna get mad."

The boy shrieked and shook her off. The cart rolled a couple of inches.

"Stop it!" said the girl.

I sidled closer, sensing imminent disaster. The boy shrieked again and reached for a potato, purply and fist sized. The cart slid another few inches, and he fell to one knee in the seat. That's when he looked at me, his eyes black and furious. He pointed a chubby finger and launched himself from the cart, landing on the floor.

I dropped the bag of apples and scooped up the howling boy as a woman with disheveled auburn hair, smeared eyeliner, and a gallon of milk rounded the corner, demanding to know what I was doing to her son.

"Ryan wouldn't sit down. He jumped out of the cart and got hurt, and the man picked him up," said the little girl. Up close, I could see that she was wearing lipstick.

"I think he broke his arm," I said to the woman. "He needs a doctor."

"Emergency room," the woman, Moira, said, and the four of us ran from the store to the parking lot as Moira frantically punched in numbers on her cell phone. "The kids' father will get us in fast," she said. "He's a doctor."

At the car, she hesitated. "We're divorced."

"You drive," I said. "I'll hold him."

"I don't even know your name," she said.

"Ben. Go."

At the hospital, the boy's howls subsided to faint moans, roving wasp eyes searching my face, fingers around my pinky in a death grip. When the doctors tried to take him from my arms to set him on the examination table, he screamed until they had to give him a sedative.

Six hours later, I came back to my mother's house empty-handed except for the phone number bunched in my fist. Dad smiled. "Oh, hello." To my mother, he said, "Who's he?"

Mom looked up from the bowl of bananas she was mashing. "That's Ben."

Dad beetled his brows. "Ben isn't that tall."

Mom finished mashing and set the bowl on the table. "So are you going to tell me about it?"

I told her. About Ryan leaping from the cart. About Ashleigh clutching the red purse. About Moira dropping the gallon of milk to the floor and accusing me of kidnapping.

"They're divorced," I said. "I mean, she's divorced. They don't seem to be managing all that well."

"It's not a good idea, Benny."

"What's not a good idea?"

She looked at my father, a man she had been planning to leave before he had the strokes. "I know you," she said.

"I don't know what you're talking about."

"You want to save those children. That mother, too."

I squeezed the scrap of paper in my hand, tried not to see my father's polite, empty smile. "Come on. I just met them."

She pressed a spoonful of mashed bananas into Dad's mouth, which he spat out. "Don't kid yourself into thinking that you're going to be their hero."

"They just needed a little help." Dad shook his head, trying, I think, to fling the banana from his chin without touching it with his hands.

She wiped Dad's face with a dish towel, giving me the same look she had given me when I was eight, when she'd found me holding vigil over a dying chipmunk the cat had used and discarded. "I know you, Benny."

Ryan sulked in the backseat of the car because I refused to turn around and go back for the inflatable dragon tube we'd bought him in Florida.

"Auntie Flo doesn't even have a pool," I said.

"I don't want it for a *pool,*" said Ryan, as if only the strange or foreign used flotation devices in pools. "I need to sit on it. This car hurts my butt."

"Oh, God," Ashleigh said. "Can't you make him shut up?"

Moira picked at her fingernails. "We're almost there, Ryan."

Ryan's hot little eyes were centered in my rearview mirror. I knew he was giving me telepathic commands to turn the car around. I squinted behind my sunglasses and used the power of my mind to fight him off.

Sometime before, I had bought a book, *Your Challenging Child,* the kind of book that promised to teach you the unteachable, like how to live peaceably with a kid that screams, "Lines! Burning lines!" for nearly twenty minutes until you figured out he was talking about the seams on his socks. On the quiz inside, Ryan tested not only as "sensitive," but also as "transitionally challenged." Have you ever noticed how many times you pass from one thing to another without even thinking about it? Ryan thought about it. We told him, "Ryan, stop building that castle, remaking your bed, riding the dog, we have to *go* now," and you saw his eyes widen and the banshees begin to howl, the way they would for him when he was thirty-five and on the train headed for work. Only then the banshees wouldn't be clamoring for his dragon tube, they would be telling him that he left the stove on in his studio apartment and his calculators would explode and his cat would be asphyxiated or at the very least several other tenants would drift into brain-creaming comas if he did not return, now, immediately.

"It's called obsessive-compulsive disorder," I told Moira.

"I thought you said he was *challenged.* I thought you said that we have to stop using such negative terms to describe him."

"A disorder isn't negative, really. We can get him some help for that."

"Oh, you'd like that, wouldn't you? He's hard for you, he's too hard for you, and you'd rather he have a disease. This way, when he throws a fit in the grocery store, you can tell the checker, 'Hey, not my fault, he's obsessive-compulsive.'"

"It *isn't* my fault. And it's gotten worse since your ex started his überdad kick a few months ago. Is he going to do this every time his girlfriend dumps him? How many amusement parks are in Illinois, anyway?"

"Stop it. You sound like a child yourself. You *want* to think Ryan's some sort of damaged goods. You want to think he's weird."

We had a deal, Moira and I. She worked as a programmer about eighty hours a week to make the vast quantities of money we enjoyed so much, and I, because my hours were the same as the kids', tended to them. I took them to school and picked them up. I brought them to the orthodontist when their teeth were growing sideways and the doctor when their fevers short-circuited the little digital thermometer. I was, consequently, invariably, the one who bore the brunt of burning lines and dragon floats, unacceptable gifts, and uningestible medicines that constituted child abuse.

"Moira," I said finally, "he *is* weird. Obsessive-compulsive is just another way of putting it."

"Really?" she said, not asking. "And which diagnosis do you think you'd qualify for?"

"What are you talking about?"

"Where do you fit in on the psychological continuum? I mean, you used to love him, right? More than me." She put up a hand when I started to protest. "A lot more than me. And now what? Four-year itch? General itch? The thrill is gone?"

"I don't know what you mean," I said.

"Sure. Sure you don't."

Ryan, in the rearview mirror: "My real daddy would have gotten my dragon tube for me."


We arrived at Auntie Flo's with Ryan still fuming but having a hard time holding on to the rage—because of my

superior will and because he was anticipating all the cup-
cakes and Jell-O and tortilla chips that Flo was literally
going to stuff him with. I, on the other hand, wanted to
punt him into the next yard.

Auntie Flo opened the door, and Ryan ran inside, screaming, "Eggs! Eggs! Eggs!" which, scrambled, is his favorite
Flo food.

Ashleigh drifted in after her brother. "You're so loud,
Ryan. Mom? Why is he so loud?"

"Don't worry about it," said Moira, putting an arm
around Flo's thin shoulders. "Auntie Flo likes things lively."

Ashleigh rolled her eyes to the whites, focused them on
one of the many renderings of the Virgin Mary Flo painted
in her spare time.

Flo lifted Ashleigh's hand and patted it. "Did you want
some eggs, too?"

"I don't eat *eggs*," said Ashleigh, her face a rictus of
teenage horror.

"Hi, Flo," I said, and pressed a kiss on her rouged cheek.
"Where's the man of the house?"

She pointed. "Where else? Drowning his sorrows in baseball."

I walked to the TV room to find Harry, Flo's husband,
shouting at the screen. "Hey there, Harry. How are you?"

"Do you believe these guys? They pay them eight million
a year and they couldn't hit a barn door. I don't believe it."

"Eight million? It's pretty incredible all right." I leaned
against the doorjamb. "So, how are you feeling?"

He shrugged. "Some days good, some days not so good."

"I hear you."

"I'm seventy-eight years old."

"I know."

"Seventy-eight years old. How am I supposed to feel? I used to weigh a hundred and ninety pounds. Now I weigh a hundred and thirty. What do you think that means?"

"I think it means that you write a diet book and make eight million bucks."

He laughed. "You said it. Eight million bucks. Do you believe these guys or what? I could have hit that pitch. And I can't even get up off this couch."

I sat in the only other chair in the tiny room, a green velvet chair with a hand-stitched doily draped over the headrest.

"Seventy-eight years old," he said. "Georgy died when he was only forty-one. What the hell kind of life is this that a father could live twice as long as his boy?"

I rested my head on the doily and thought about my father, who had essentially been playing at dying for years. He told the same story over and over again, mostly to young women he met while walking the dog: "I had this great therapist over at the rehab center. Sally Klagenhorn. She was so pretty. Then she got married. You know what her new name was? Sally Keister. Get it? Keister! And she had a nice one, too!" When he started grabbing the keisters of the poor young women who took pity on him, my mother started walking the dog.

Uncle Harry, a large, gregarious man who had spent forty years of his life delivering mail for the post office, always ready to talk with anyone about anything, had shrunk suddenly, in size and spirit, almost instantly the day his only son, Georgy, died of melanoma three years before. Now, Uncle Harry had two topics: the demise of baseball and his own demise. One thing lamented, the other courted.

"It's a terrible thing when a man outlives his son," I said.

He shook his head. "Nobody should live this long. It ain't natural. Sometimes I can't feel my feet. I have to look down to see if they're still there."

Moira peeked her head into the Florida room. "You two need anything?" She looked from me to Harry and back to me again, one eyebrow raised slightly. I was supposed to be convincing Harry to see a doctor about cancer treatment options, and Moira would expect an update on my progress soon enough.

Harry continued to stare at the TV screen, so I answered for both of us. "No, Harry and I are fine just as we are."

Harry grunted, eyeglasses dancing with little pin-striped men. "That's a sin. It's just a sin, plain and simple."

"Who's that?" said Moira. She was looking out the front window at a bottle green station wagon crawling into the driveway. A woman got out of the driver's side and opened the back door. A small boy climbed out from the back, absently but skillfully throwing a yo-yo.

"That's Shakti," said Harry.

"Who's Shakti?" I said. "*What's* Shakti?"

"Shakti. Georgy's girl," said Harry. "That's her boy, AJ. Nice kid. Quiet as a damn mouse, though."

"You mean the woman who . . ." Moira trailed off, searching. "The woman he was with right before he died?"

"You never met Shakti? I thought you met her at Easter."

Moira plucked imaginary lint from the folds of her skirt. "No, Uncle Harry. Never had the pleasure."

"Oh, you're going to like her, Moira. She's just great. She

still calls every Sunday morning like clockwork. A real sweetheart."

Moira didn't look as if she were prepared to think this Shakti was much of a sweetheart. "What about Trish?"

"Oh, we still talk to Trish. Not as much, to tell you the truth."

"Why not?"

"Where was she when Georgy got sick?" said Harry. "Shakti had to quit her job to take care of him."

Moira pursed her lips and stared out the window, struggling mightily, I thought, not to remind her uncle exactly who had been fucking around on whom, something that was very important to Moira, even if the guilty party was her cousin, had died young and tragically, and, it could be argued, was receiving his just rewards as we spoke.

Shakti and her son had taken a platter of cookies from the trunk of the car and were making their way up the front steps. We could hear Auntie Flo greet them through the thin walls.

"Hello! Hello! Come on in. Everyone's already here."

"Oh, Flo! It's great to see you! You look wonderful. AJ, say hello to Aunt Flo. . . . AJ?"

"Oh, don't bother him now. Boys his age don't have much use for old ladies like me, right, AJ? There's chips and soda in the kitchen if you want some. I can make you some eggs later."

Flo and Shakti appeared in the door of the Florida room. Flo took Moira's arm. "You two remember each other, don't you?"

Shakti offered, "Of course," just as Moira said, "I don't think so." The two women smiled at each other slightly, Shakti's quizzical, Moira's as inscrutable as a virus.

"No?" said Shakti. From the name, I had expected an Indian woman, but Shakti was pale and small and freckled, with long straight brown hair she wore parted down the middle.

"I'm sorry, I thought we had met. I've seen a lot of pictures, I guess," Shakti said. "And Flo talks about you all the time."

"That must be it," Moira said, standing up straighter so that she could sharpen the angle between her eyes and Shakti's.

"I feel like I already know you."

"Really?"

Before Moira could really start putting on the freeze, Ryan let go one of his legendary shrieks, one that could have deafened us all even if we had been sealed in an iron box and buried under the driveway.

I muttered, "What now?" and earned a look of hurt and contempt from Moira, who turned and dashed out of the room, followed by everyone but Harry, who remained in his seat to witness the various athletic atrocities committed by his favorite team.

"Oh, I hope nobody's hurt," Shakti said as we power-walked toward the kitchen.

"I hope we don't have to hurt anybody," I replied. We found Ashleigh flipping through one of Auntie Flo's fashion magazines, circa 1962, Moira cleaning up an overturned plateful of scrambled eggs, Ryan red faced and pointing at AJ. AJ was standing in the corner by the back door of the house, throwing his yo-yo, his back to the kitchen table.

"AJ? What happened?" Shakti said.

"Your son wanted some eggs," Moira said. "So he took some from Ryan's plate."

"Oh, I'm sorry!" Shakti said. "AJ, you should apologize to the little boy."

"He stole my eggs!" screamed Ryan. "Those were *my* eggs! Auntie Flo made them for *me.*"

"Oh, Ryan, calm down. It's not that big a deal," I said.

"It's a big deal to me!"

"What *isn't* a big deal to you?" I walked over to the table and started gathering egg pellets from its surface.

"Why do you always talk to him like that?" said Moira. "He has no idea what you're talking about."

"Ryan, do you know what I'm talking about?"

"My eggs are all over the floor!"

"Don't worry, honey, I'll make you some more eggs," said Auntie Flo. "And I'll make AJ some, too."

I watched AJ for his reaction to this charming family drama. He didn't even turn around.

Shakti grabbed a sponge and began wiping the surface of the table. Ashleigh lifted her magazine so she could wipe underneath. Moira glared when Shakti accidentally hit her in the arm with the wet sponge, and Moira, dangerously, opened her mouth to speak.

"Tell you what," I said. "Why don't we all have some eggs? I think we could use the protein."

Later, out in the yard, I strolled around the perimeter of the prodigious garden with Doris, Flo's ancient cat, observing as she stopped to smell this or that blossom. Every once in a while she would sit down and watch as a bee sailed from the nucleus of a flower, pointing at it with her nose the way we might with a finger. It was only after I watched her do this several times that I realized Doris believed the bees were trapped inside the flowers and that she was the only one with the power to release them.

"Cool cat."

I turned around. Shakti was standing there, head tilted slightly so that her brown hair hung like a curtain from the top of her ear. Her thin dress clung to the tips of her breasts.

"Yes," I said. "She is a cool cat." Doris strolled over and rubbed my legs so that I would stoop down and pet her, which I did. "A great cat. I love this cat."

"I'm sorry about what AJ did."

"Please. Don't worry about it. He's a kid. And Ryan is spoiled."

"Like you said, he's a kid."

I closed my eyes for a second, wondering if my resentment was that obvious. "Yes, you're right. He makes me so angry sometimes that I forget that. Moira has to remind me."

"Moira's beautiful."

"Yes, she is."

"And fierce. A warrior." She pumped both fists.

I laughed. "That too."

"She's angry at me because of Georgy, I know that. But Trish and Georgy were having problems before I came along. They weren't sleeping together. Trish didn't love him anymore, you know."

From the look on Shakti's face, I didn't think that she believed Georgy's line anymore, but it was important that she keep toeing it.

"It doesn't matter," I said. "People only see what they want to see. Or what they need to see."

"We need villains."

I was startled. "What did you say?"

"Villains. And heroes. Good people against bad."

I couldn't help but smile. "Ah, but they're not exactly 'bad,' I said, "they're *sick.*"

"Oh, yes," said Shakti. "You're right. *Sick.*" She tucked her hair behind a small, shell-like ear. "That's another thing I've seen a lot of. Sickness."

"Are you a doctor?"

"A colon therapist." She wandered over to the flower bed, tipped a tall blossom toward her face, but didn't sniff it. "I opened a clinic after Georgy died."

"I'm afraid to ask what a colon therapist is."

"The colon is the part of the body that no one wants to speak about, that everyone wants to ignore. Until they're eating a bottle of Tums every day. I offer nutritional counseling, massage therapy, and colon irrigation for the relief of those kinds of problems."

"Bellyaches, you mean."

"Did you know that the colon mirrors the way that you live?"

"Um. No, I didn't."

"It does. Why do you think there's so much colon cancer in this country?"

"Too many big steaks?" I asked.

She nodded. "That, and repression. All these angry people, working too hard, stressed out. But no one knows how to talk about stress. They don't know how to let go of it. The hurt stays inside."

"Uh-huh," I said. I found myself wishing for another egg disaster.

"So," she said. "What do you do?"

"I'm a teacher. Fifth grade."

"Really? That must be wonderful. All that positive energy."

"They've got energy all right," I said. "Kids are never so confident as they are when they're ten and eleven. They think they can rule the world. They think they can fly."

She raised an eyebrow. "And I guess it's your job to ground them?"

"They still get skinned knees. They still cry. It can't all be Batman and Catwoman." I shuffled my feet, and I hate when people shuffle their feet. "I don't mind. Really, that's the best part. Fixing them up so that they can go back to being superheroes again."

"Do you suffer from constipation, Ben?"

"Excuse me?"

"Constipation."

I blinked. There it was, the diagnosis. Moira would have been grimly pleased to hear it, even if it was medical rather than psychological. "This isn't usually a topic at family gatherings."

"I'm guessing the answer is yes. Do you know why?"

"I'm very angry?" I said. *Shakti,* I thought. *Her name's probably Susan. Or Maryann.*

Susan-Maryann-Shakti gave me a small Mona Lisa. "What goes in must come out," she said. "You can't hold back what you really feel. Emotional holding can cause physical distress. Acne. Bad breath. Dry skin. Leaky gut."

I looked at her pale skin, her thin hair. What had happened to her? Who was AJ's father? Not Georgy; the boy

was as brown as Shiva. "I guess you don't suffer from constipation."

"My name means a lot of things, but one of them is energy," she said, "sexual and otherwise. I need release." She
lifted her chin a notch. "I don't let things build up. I say
what I need to say. I do what I need to do."

I wondered whether this need-to-do had included Georgy,
who was married at the time. "Is Shakti your given name?"

"The one I've given myself."

*Please.* "You didn't answer my question. How's *your*
plumbing?"

She smiled that elliptical smile again and then held up
her hands, fingers together but thumbs splayed, in two
L-shapes that mirrored each other. She brought her hands up
to frame her face, her chin resting on her thumbs.

I was in no mood for charades, but I've always been one
for saying what people want to hear. "Pretty as a picture."

Her smile broadened into a grin, then she dropped her
hands. "The truth is in the toilet."


I wasn't much of a dater before Moira. The singles world
seemed to be populated with wan, ambivalent types, end-
lessly analyzing if they were ready for love, for marriage, for
mortgages and mommy clothes. I couldn't help but feel an
almost obnoxious smugness when we'd had Ashleigh's
boyfriend, Devin, and his parents over for dinner. Devin's father was reasonable enough, but his stepmother, Lu, was all
sarcasm and stringy muscles humming with stress and bewilderment. Watching Devin pile his plate with broccoli—
and only broccoli—Lu had crossed her arms tight around her

chest, as if willing her innards to stay in. "I went through a vegetarian phase, too. Every kid goes through one. I guess."

So I was grateful for Moira, for her certitude, for her insistence that everything she does is somehow related to the fact that she is Irish, for her claims that she had nothing whatsoever to do with the demise of her first marriage, for her ferocity, and for her wit. And then the kids—evidence of that certitude—wide, frightened eyes, smooth heads I could cup in the palm of my hand. I was so hugely thankful for them, their power, which made my own heart swell, their wounds, which I could kiss away. At our wedding, in the moment I watched Ryan light a candle for us all, I was even grateful to his father, for being the kind of man who considers children merely an homage to their mother, for bowing out and letting us blend in the best sense of that tepid word.

But I guess he never intended to bow out for good, and he'd linger just long enough to do the most damage. And I was the ambivalent one, unclear, unsure. All I knew was that when Moira went out of town on business, the children stayed with him. It was Moira's presence that made me a parent. Without her, what was I?

"Did you talk to Harry?" Moira asked me, leaning over my shoulder as I tried to wash a glass in the kitchen sink.

"I tried," I said. I had made my way back into Harry's haunt, wondering despite myself whether I really was emotionally "irregular," so to speak. All I'd managed to do was murmur the word *hospital,* the word *treatment.* As feeble as he was, the look on Harry's face would have scared the shit right out of anybody, no matter how constipated. He'd held up a finger that arthritis had clearly had its wanton way with and said: "The only thing the doctors can prescribe for me is a gun."

"He's not going for it," I said.

Her lips tightened into a pinkish seam. "Then you've got to try again."

"Moira, he's seventy-eight years old. He doesn't want chemotherapy. He doesn't want radiation. He wants to watch baseball. Is that so wrong?"

She threw down the dish towel she was holding. "Yes, it's wrong," she said. "This is my uncle we're talking about. And he has a chance to—"

"To what?" I asked. "To try out for the Olympics? To join chat groups on the Internet? To take up country-western dancing?"

She jabbed her finger at me. "He still has a couple of good years ahead of him."

Doris padded into the kitchen and wound around my legs. I thought of my mother, my father. Some things are just too far gone. "Moira," I said, her name a sigh, "this isn't about you."

She jerked away from me as if I had shoved her. "How can you say that?" she said. "How can you?"

I answered honestly, just as surprised as she was. "I don't know."


The party, such as it was, migrated to the small living room, which was painted a loud robin's-egg blue. I was slouched in the doorway between it and the kitchen, attempting to appear relaxed and casual. Ashleigh was slumped—bored and not afraid of showing it—in an overstuffed La-Z-Boy. On the couch, Moira and Shakti sat, upper bodies tilting away from each other as if their heads were opposing magnets. AJ was crowded at the very end of the couch, wedged between a pillow and the armrest, his yo-yo still on his lap. Ryan sat at AJ's bare feet, gazing up at him.

"Want to play a game?" Ryan asked.

AJ didn't answer. I looked to Shakti, watched her bite her lip.

"Hey, you," said Ryan.

"His name is AJ, honey," said Moira.

"His real name is Ajit," Shakti said, eliciting a peculiar low growling from AJ. "But he prefers AJ. Obviously. It means invincible. Little Buddha." Shakti smoothed her dress over her knees, releasing energy more nervous than sexual. "He's so invincible that he won't let me call him invincible."

Ryan was on a mission. "I *said,* do you want to play a game?"

AJ turned his head, blinked slowly, as if his eyelids were weighted with nickels. His fingers fluttered over the yo-yo.

A mother with a personal philosophy of self-expression raises a son as expressive as a houseplant. Who was this woman? I thought. A nurse from Indiana? A hygienist from Kansas? Who were we all kidding, anyway?

I felt a sudden tenderness toward the mute boy. "AJ doesn't like to talk much, Ryan."

"Yeah, Ryan, why don't you leave the kid alone, okay?" Ashleigh said. I glanced at her, and she scowled and tried to sink farther into the chair.

"Does anyone want more eggs?" Auntie Flo wanted to know. "Or pop? I have pop in the fridge."

"How many eggs can a person eat?" Ashleigh grumbled

into her cleavage. "Mom, don't forget Dad's picking us up in an hour, okay? So we're going to leave soon, right?"

Ryan stared openly at AJ, brows furrowing. I could see the rage that wormed into his expression, the embarrassment that pinkened his skin. *I'm sorry, Ryan,* I thought. *I* am.

Ryan reached out with his little fingers and pinched one of AJ's big toes. "Hey, *you!*"

AJ jumped up from the couch, yo-yo flying, and ran right out the door before any of us could draw in a breath to speak.

I guess these things are in my blood, in my bones, because I leapt from my perch in the doorway and ran out after him. He'd made it only as far as the end of the driveway when I lunged, reaching out my arms and grabbing his elbows from behind, pulled him sideways. We fell onto Auntie Flo's lawn.

AJ's legs pinwheeled wildly, catching me in the shins once, twice. Pissed, I gripped harder, forcing his face into the grass, *dumb kid, another stupid, pain-in-the-ass kid.* His breaths came out in hard, almost tangible pants, and I could feel his wiry little-boy muscles bucking and straining. His goal wasn't to surprise us. He meant to keep going.

As we struggled, I saw the group of them, my slapdash family, pouring from the house like some furious froth of insects. The knowledge that I was just filling in the holes left by someone else, that we could not keep one another safe, they could leave me, and I them, hit me and sent me reeling.

Now, years later, I see them differently, I see what I could not have seen. Ashleigh, wide-eyed and flushed, interested in something other than the mysteries of her own body for the first time in months. Ryan, his essential hurt radiating like bands of light. Moira, the terrible fear that fed her certainty.

But then, as I wrestled with this strange boy, this unknowable, unfathomable boy, I wrestled them all. *I can fix you if you let me. And in the fixing, I will be, too.* One of AJ's elbows caught me in the teeth. My mouth filled with blood, and I shook my head in surprise. My grip around the boy's arms slackened, broke. He rolled gracefully to his bare feet and for a moment looked down upon me like some minor god. Then he turned tail and ran. I flexed my empty hands and could only guess when—if—the spirit would move him to return.

# I'M NOT JULIA ROBERTS

They decided to meet in neutral territory, the diner with the neon baked potato blinking over the door. They had spoken before, of course, at soccer games and school functions, disapproving front doors where they handed off the children; but up to now, their talk was nothing more than empty, guarded. And they could have met somewhere else to break through their personal Berlin Wall, someone's kitchen, say, or someone's living room, but neither wanted "that woman" in her house, lurking around like a bargain-basement spy. Still, they must have clung to some belief, some vague hope of exchange or resolution, to bring them to this odd, anonymous place, where a busboy, stooped as a gargoyle, pushed a choked dust mop across the floor.

Beatrix sat on one side of a booth, nursing a cup of coffee, as Lu slid into the other side. Lu's face and hair were peppered with droplets of water.

"I guess it's raining," said Beatrix.

"It just started." Lu glanced at the busboy and his mop. "I think that guy has enough dust to knit himself a cat." She snatched up a napkin and blotted her brow.

"All the weather reports said rain today. Did you listen to the reports?" Beatrix had a collapsible black umbrella hanging on the hook next to her seat. When Lu didn't respond, she said, "Are you going to want coffee?"

"Do I need it?" said Lu.

"I don't know. Do you?" said Beatrix, and looked away, out the rain-glazed window, not bothering to point out their server.

The waitress, a skinny girl-woman far too pretty for her surroundings or her brown polyester uniform, appeared at their table with a menu. Lu barely glanced at it. "I'd like coffee? And a piece of apple pie?" When Lu was really tense, she sometimes turned statements into questions, like a teenager.

"Absolutely," said the waitress. Rather than stare at each other, rather than begin what was guaranteed to be an unpleasant or at least uncomfortable business, Beatrix and Lu watched as the waitress walked toward the counter, yanked a coffeepot off a burner, and circled back to her customers. She filled Lu's cup and plunked a handful of creamers onto the table. "I'll be right back with the pie."

"Thanks," Lu said. She opened one of the creamers and sniffed it.

Beatrix waited until Lu had doctored her coffee with three creamers and two packets of sugar. "So," she began.

"So," said Lu. Beatrix was armed with a notepad, a pen, and a short stack of manila folders. Ward, Lu's husband and

Beatrix's ex, had warned Lu about the folders. He said that Beatrix kept every receipt, every letter, every Christmas card, every cocktail napkin decorated with drunken witticisms, filed in these folders. If you stupidly forgot something you'd written to her decades before, she would pull out a random valentine and read aloud to refresh your memory. Lu was glad that she'd never written Beatrix, even though she had been sorely tempted, mostly by words running to four letters.

"I guess you know why I asked you to meet me," Beatrix continued.

"No," said Lu. "I don't." Sweat prickled on her upper lip, which hadn't yet achieved the stiffness she desired and probably never would. Out of the blue, Beatrix had decided that it might be easier to communicate with Lu than with Ward. Though it was not her job, and though Beatrix had sent some serious missiles Lu's way, Lu found herself agreeing to try. She had gotten more and more concerned with the way Ward was handling his ex; he might as well have been writing his letters in Farsi for all Beatrix seemed to understand them. And then there was the fact that while Ward made a big manly show of putting his foot down, he seldom did. It wouldn't have surprised Lu if she came home one day to find their stuff packed up in boxes on the lawn. *Well, Beatrix thinks it would be best for the kids if we sold our house, gave her all the money, and spent the next ten years in a pup tent in her backyard. I know it sucks, honey, but what can I do?*

Beatrix tapped the pen against the notepad impatiently. "It's about time that we stop beating around the bush and get some things settled."

"Uh-huh," said Lu. She took a sip of her coffee, making a show of calm. *Beating around the bush? I'll give you beating around the bush.* She tried to employ her yoga breathing, then remembered that all the yoga training she'd ever had was the one tape, and did you really need a tape to learn how to breathe? Wasn't this yet another sign of their disposable and frivolous culture?

*No,* she thought. I'm *a sign of that disposable and frivolous culture.* Shake a broken family long enough and out falls the trophy wife. Except that wasn't technically true, either. She was too old, too dark, too thin in the lips. But that didn't stop people from jumping to their own salacious conclusions. Glynn, Lu's new friend, had hinted that perhaps if Lu had had an affair with Ward, and perhaps if this was what broke up Ward's first marriage, it explained why Beatrix seemed so hostile.

"No!" Lu had shouted. "I didn't!"

"You wouldn't be the first," Glynn had said gently.

"But I didn't!"

"I'm sorry. I was just trying to find a reason."

Now, Beatrix removed a piece of paper from one of the folders. She slid it across the table to Lu. "This is for Ward."

"What is it?"

"A doctor's bill."

"I see that," said Lu. "Which doctor? I don't recognize the name."

"A specialist. For Britt. I don't like his eye."

"Pardon me?" said Lu.

"His eye. Haven't you noticed that his right eye floats into his nose when he looks to his left?" Lu's own eyes widened, and Beatrix sighed. "He has a lazy eye. There's something wrong with the muscle. He probably needs surgery."

"Is that what the doctor said?"

Beatrix hesitated. The doctor had said that while Britt's eye was a bit wonky, he didn't think surgery was necessary. *Wonky.* Suddenly the whole stupid world was talking like Harry Potter. "I'm getting a second opinion," she told Lu. "Anyway, Ward needs to pay half this bill."

"Okay," said Lu. She folded the bill and laid it at the end of the table, next to the condiments. "I'll give it to him."

"See that he pays it immediately," Beatrix said.

"I'll give it to him." Lu opened another creamer and dumped it into her cup. "Whatever happened with Ollie's leg?"

Beatrix stiffened. "There's a technical name for how his legs are shaped."

"A little knock-kneed?" Lu offered.

"No. Something else. Severe cases sometimes require—"

"Surgery. I know."

The waitress came with Lu's apple pie, crumb topped, and the two women leaned back in their seats, grateful for the brief respite. Beatrix watched Lu pluck a fat crumb from the top of the pie and pop it into her mouth. She had to force herself not to slap the woman's hand. Here was the reason her sons' table manners were going to hell. And why had she ordered *pie*? What was this, snack time? Weren't they meeting to talk? To get things settled?

Because there *were* things to settle. Many things. Like, for instance, why Ollie, her youngest, had suddenly refused to go to his father's house, why an eleven-year-old boy lay down on the floor and wailed like a starving newborn when Ward came to pick him up. Loopy—the stupid pet name her boys called Lu—looked at him funny, Ollie had confessed to Beatrix. He didn't want to go to places where people looked at him funny. It made him think they hated him. It gave him weird dreams.

The waitress hadn't left yet. "This a business meeting?"

"Sorry?" said Beatrix.

"You two. You look like you're all business." She tapped the pile of manila folders with an enthusiastically manicured fingernail. "We don't get many like you in here."

"Oh?" Lu said politely. "What do you usually get?"

"I don't know," the girl-woman said. "All types. Families, mostly." She gestured vaguely to the next booth, where a man and a woman were eating cheese omelets in silence, a small boy gleefully ramming a butter knife through his paper placemat.

"That's nice," said Lu, not looking at Beatrix. She had read a book that said that first and second wives have to make a huge effort to get along, as they are, in a sense, kin, a new kind of family. Lu had found this book rather disturbing. Though she herself had married a man with children, she still wanted to believe that families were little more than crazy, unavoidable accidents—*Whoops, there it is!* And then there was the fact that peacekeeping was always up to the women. Why was everything always up to the women? Fathers and stepfathers grunted at each other, perhaps bellowed at each other once or twice over the phone or brawled on somebody's lawn, but they never had to meet for coffee. Lu had wanted to shout at the book: Men don't drink coffee??

The waitress held up the coffeepot as if there might be

more cups to fill. Then she said, "Well, just call me if you need anything else. My name's Heather."

"Heather," said Lu.

"Okay," Beatrix said, staring at Heather till she stalked off, the pot banging into her hip as she walked.

"I'm concerned about Ollie," Beatrix said.

Lu wiped her hands on her napkin. "Yes. Me too."

"You," Beatrix said with reptilian flatness. "What are your feelings for my child?"

"Excuse me?" Lu gave a little laugh. "What do you mean?" She'd recently been thrown off an electronic message board, secondwivesspeakeasy.com, for suggesting that not every stepmother falls madly in love with her stepkids on sight, and vice versa, and that she couldn't quite believe the women who said that they did. At least, that was the excuse the moderators used. The real reason they threw her off the board, Lu believed, was the fact that she had dared to mock the movie *Stepmom,* a wildly unrealistic and weepy favorite with the second wife set. Lu thought that it was because Julia Roberts had played the beleaguered stepmother, and didn't every stepmother secretly aspire to be Julia Roberts, well scrubbed and well-meaning, the girl next door with the big smile and bigger heart? "First of all," Lu had posted in a particularly weak moment, "the movie is set in some fantasy New York Cityland where there is *no traffic.* Ever. Second, the bio-mom gets cancer and DIES in that idiotic movie. Who here is going to get that lucky?"

"It means you need to explain your feelings for my son. He seems to think that you hate him."

"He what?" Lu said.

"Do I need to write it down for you?"

"You asked me to come here. I can leave if you'd prefer to be alone."

Beatrix exhaled through her nose. "I just want to know what's going on. He told me that you look at him funny, that you don't like him or want him around. That's why he refuses to go to your house."

Lu's mouth dropped open. "That's what he told you? 'Cause he told me that he didn't want to come over because we don't have a Sony PlayStation."

Beatrix didn't speak for a full ten seconds. Then she said, "Are you saying my son's a liar?"

"I'm saying that he might be telling you what you'd like to hear."

"Maybe that's what he's telling *you*," Beatrix snapped.

"Okay," said Lu.

"Okay, what?"

"Okay, okay," Lu said. "It's obvious he's telling you one thing and telling us another. And that's not the worst of his problems. He's a big boy—"

"He is not!"

"I meant that he's *not* a little boy, *not* a baby, and he's still throwing temper tantrums that would make a toddler green with envy. If you hadn't whipped him out of therapy—"

"I didn't *whip* him out," said Beatrix. "Who said I did that? Ward could have taken him if he thought it was important. Anyway, that therapist was a quack. He had us all doing homework, for God's sake. Like I don't get enough work at work! I don't need to be filling out charts and handing out bribes. It's ridiculous."

"So much for discussion," Lu muttered. With a fork, she stabbed at her pie, not caring that the crumbs showered into her lap. It had been years now, and sometimes, sometimes, the boys were alien to her, like some lost tribe who'd never seen a wheel or a spoon, like bugs with which you could speak. As soon as it seemed that they were lurching toward something real—if not love, then something like it, a delicate affection, a shy sort of fondness—they moved into another possessed-by-demons phase and Lu felt the ground shift beneath her.

Avoiding Beatrix's angry, splotchy face, Lu observed the people at the next booth. There, the mother and the father continued to chew as placidly as ruminants as their son bloodied his torn placemat with giant blobs of ketchup. She wondered what those parents felt about their son, if, at that very moment, they were thinking of him as an infant, how his little baby head had smelled of powder and musk, how his laughter had sounded like the distant chime of bells.

The waitress floated by again, a spray of silverware in one hand. "That's a nice shirt," she said, nodding at Beatrix. "Where'd you get it?"

Beatrix frowned even more deeply than she had been, fingering the cloth of her shiny green blouse. "A catalog."

"Oh yeah? Which one?"

"I don't remember."

"Oh," said the waitress. "I'd like to get a shirt like that. My mom got engaged, and we're having a party for her. Just a house party, but me and my sister want it to be nice. Dressed up, you know?"

"Congratulations," Lu said.

The waitress looked at her. "For what?"

"On your mom's engagement. I mean, if that's a good thing. For her or you or anyone."

"Yeah, thanks," said the waitress, tucking a fringe of bleached hair behind her ear. She glanced from Lu to Beatrix. "You want a piece of pie? It's good. They make it fresh every morning."

"No, thank you," said Beatrix.

"Watching your weight, huh?" Heather the Waitress said. "Me too."

Beatrix stared at the skinny, skinny girl. "I don't like *pie.*"

"Oh," said Heather, looking as if she had just been hit in the face by a cobweb. "Well. I'll be at the counter if you want me."

"Good for you." Beatrix flipped open one of the folders and paged through her notes and letters. The smell of the pie was driving her nuts; she'd just started Atkins, and the coffee alone was a huge no-no. She couldn't afford to eat pie, too. It made her furious that Lu was eating it. She wasn't so thin, either. At least, not as thin as she'd been when Ward started parading her around as if she were the prom queen.

At least Lu was close to Beatrix's age. So many other first wives she knew had to deal with second wives like Heather the Waitress, emaciated little twits not even twenty-five, teetering around in too high heels and too tight jeans, acting as if life hadn't officially begun until they strutted through the door. Please. Beatrix remembered her early twenties quite well, thank you, remembered the cluelessness, the shallowness, the head-up-the-assness. Wasn't that when she'd chosen to marry Ward? Didn't that prove that no one should be allowed to get married before the age of thirty?

*There should be laws,* thought Beatrix, *there should be rules and requirements and guidelines. No second wives under twenty-*

*five, no second wives who looked like movie stars.* Here, Beatrix had lucked out. Lu was no Julia Roberts.

Lu was again examining the doctor's bill that she had tossed next to the sugar packets and mustard, her expression unreadable. *What?* Beatrix thought. *I'm not allowed to take my son to a specialist when it's perfectly clear that there's something wrong with his eye? I'm not allowed to emphasize that payment should be made immediately when Ward's concept of "immediately" seems to be "if and when I feel like it so get off my case"?*

She wondered what, if anything, she was allowed to do in Lu's opinion. Thank Lu for making her youngest feel fat and unwelcome in his own father's house? Thank her for trying to purchase her oldest son's affections with expensive jeans and gym shoes? Thank her for going to her middle son's afternoon sporting events—events that Beatrix could not possibly attend because she had a regular nine-to-five—and making Beatrix look like an uncaring, unsupportive hag? *Rules!* she thought. *Rules!*

Beatrix felt the anger like a spike through the top of her head, the heat of it racing through her veins, and she took a gulp of water. She would kill for her kids—any mother would—but she didn't like being so intimate with that knowledge.

The gargoyle busboy sidled by the table, smelling of smoke and Parmesan. He waved his hand at Lu's plate. "Finished?" he mumbled.

Lu pushed the plate with the half-eaten piece of pie toward the edge of the table. "If I'm not, I probably should be."

Out of the corner of her eye, Lu could see Beatrix fussing with her files again, her lips in a tight, sour pucker. She was sure Beatrix felt judged, and judged lacking, by Lu, and while that was true, it was also true that Lu didn't want Beatrix's job. In Ward, Lu had found that rarest of things: the nearly perfect husband. He loved her so well when he was around and yet went on business trips just long enough and often enough to convince her that she hadn't lost herself completely, hadn't turned into a bubble-headed, tittering wifey-wife the way some of her old friends had, or a seething bitch who complained constantly about how unappreciated she was, like some of her other friends. Yet this satisfaction didn't trickle down to the kids, not in the triple-exclamation-point way all those women on secondwives-speakeasy.com claimed it did ("I like to call my stepchildren my *bonus* children!!!"). It might have been normal to feel differently about the boys, but it didn't feel right. It was like trying not to stare at a person with a prosthetic arm: You worked so hard not to focus on the arm that it was all you could think about. Prosthetic arms everywhere.

Lu sighed. Just once, she would like to have a triple-exclamation-point moment. "Other than his eye, Britt seems to be doing better."

"Britt was just tossed off the tennis team for throwing a racket at the umpire."

"Besides that," Lu said.

"Besides that?"

"Yeah," Lu said. "He's a funny kid, don't you think?"

Beatrix didn't know how to respond to this comment. "Sometimes he could try being a little less funny."

"But then he wouldn't be Britt." Lu hated herself for the chirpy tone of her voice, but she couldn't help it. She was simply not normal around this woman.

"Yes," said Beatrix, rolling her eyes. "I suppose not." She paused. "What about Devin? How's he doing?"

"Okay." Lu realized that she should probably say more, as both of them knew that Devin had been avoiding his mother ever since he came to live with his father. This might have made Lu feel superior if Devin hadn't calcified into some walking statue of teenage blankness and rage, and if that walking statue wasn't perched in Lu's living room every day, staring stonily at the TV. But then, there were cracks here and there. She'd seen them. And besides, Lu believed that Devin had moved in with his father not because Ward was a better parent, but because Devin wanted to torture him up close and personal.

This was not what she told Beatrix, however. "It's hard to tell with Devin," Lu said carefully. "You know he doesn't say that much. I think he's . . . better."

The corners of Beatrix's mouth twitched. "Is he still dating that girl?"

"Ashleigh?" said Lu. "Unfortunately."

"Aren't you friendly with her mother?"

"Just because I like Moira," said Lu, tugging at her collar, "doesn't mean I like her kid. Every time I see Ashleigh I want to tell her to tuck her boobs back into her shirt."

"Maybe you should," said Beatrix.

"That'd be nice."

"No, really. She looks like that singer, what's her name? The one who can't sing but distracts everyone by falling out of her clothes."

"You could be describing one of dozens of people. Hundreds, maybe. Entire junior highs full of kids. Grade school kids are wearing *Sesame Street* thongs."

"Well, anyway, who knows where it will lead?"

Lu nodded. "I know."

"I'm talking about Ashleigh. A girl with clothes like that. I bet she has a *collection* of thongs. . . ." Beatrix trailed off, raising her eyebrows.

"Lots of girls who don't wear thongs," Lu said, "do all sorts of stuff that their moms wouldn't approve of. Besides, isn't that something you should discuss with Devin? Boys are just as accountable for their behavior as girls are."

"We wouldn't have any trouble if they were properly supervised," said Beatrix.

Lu's blink came in stages. "Supervised."

"I have to explain this to you?" Beatrix barked.

"What do you want? Cameras in his backpack? We can only supervise them so much." Lu used her index and middle fingers to put quotation marks around the word *supervise.* "We can't be with them every minute of every day. We can only present them with the facts. We have to hope and trust that they'll be responsible."

"*Hope* that they'll be responsible? How about *demand* that they be responsible?"

"Hope, demand, expect. When it comes down to it, they're going to do what they're going to do."

Beatrix's face tightened into a mask. "That's a perfectly insane way to think about this issue. But I'm not surprised to hear this from you."

Lu grabbed for her fork, then remembered her place had been cleared. "Oh, God. Do they serve alcohol here?"

"I don't appreciate the way that the subject of sex was introduced to my sons."

"Maybe I'll order myself a whole pie."

"If you and Ward hadn't spent so much time carrying on in front of my children, maybe they wouldn't have so many problems. Maybe Devin wouldn't have gotten so many ideas." Beatrix's finger came down like a jackhammer upon the pile of folders, as if she already had all the evidence she'd ever need.

Lu watched the jackhammering finger, remembered a night in which Britt had come upon Lu and Ward kissing. *It was just* kissing. *We should outlaw kissing?* "I don't even know what you're talking about. I never did. And speaking about carrying on, how about what you and Alan were doing?" Lu attempted to make more quotation marks, but her hands slashed at the air, like a person having a seizure. "Don't you think that might have given the boys some, uh, ideas? And don't you think they would have gotten ideas no matter what you or Ward or your husband or I did?"

Beatrix wiped the table with a napkin. "I guess some people," she continued as if Lu hadn't spoken, "don't like to take responsibility for what they've done."

"You got that right," Lu said. This was her life now, a life of revisionist history, marked by petty skirmishes over bills, curfews, meals, clothes, visitation, TV, computer time, housework, holidays, even residences. How long could she tough it out? How long till she punched the next sanctimonious jerk-off who said: You *knew* he had kids; you *knew* what you were getting into.

Heather the Waitress hovered, her skinny little arms behind her back. "Do you guys want anything else? More coffee or anything?"

"No, thank you," Beatrix told her. Lu merely shook her head in unconscious defeat.

"Okay, then. Here's your check." The waitress turned and almost crashed into the little boy, the one from the next table who had been so artfully mutilating his placemat. In his hands he held a stiff piece of toast on which was balanced a pepper shaker.

"Whoa!" said Heather.

"Dakota, get back here, you're going to break that," his mother said. She stood and zipped up her brown hoodie sweatshirt to her neck. "Leave those ladies alone."

The little boy grinned as he set down the toast and shaker on Lu's side of the table. "Meat!" he said.

"Maybe in another dimension. Here, it's just pepper," Lu told him, taking the shaker off the toast and placing it on the table. Beatrix scowled, though it wasn't obvious whether she was displeased with Lu or the boy or both.

The boy's mother crouched behind him. "Say good-bye to the nice ladies."

"Meat," snarled the boy.

At the next table, the boy's father laid a twenty on top of his check. He smiled sheepishly, lips pink and womanly in his white face. "He calls everything meat now. We don't know why. Last month it was 'bug.' Everything was 'bug.' You'd say 'hi,' he'd say 'bug.' Kids are crazy."

"Crazy," agreed Beatrix. "You said it."

Lu sneezed abruptly, like a dog.

"Say good-bye, Dakota," his mother insisted.

"Dakota!" said Dakota.

Dakota's mother sighed, then swung the boy onto her hip. Her perfume wafted over Beatrix and Lu's table, a mommy scent, cloying and heavy and sweet. "Sorry for interrupting your visit," she said. "Are you two sisters?"

Heather the Hovering Waitress took a tiny step forward. "I was just thinking that. You have the same kind of, um, *way* about you. The same . . . what's that word? I just learned it in psych class . . . oh! Gestalt."

That did it. Beatrix scooped up the check before Lu could get it and before Heather the Waitress could expound further.

"Let me," Lu said. "I had the pie."

"No, no. This was my idea." Beatrix opened her wallet and fished for a ten, which she gave to Heather the Waitress.

"I'll get your change," Heather said.

Beatrix gathered up her folders and her umbrella. "You keep the change."

"Thanks!" Heather said. "Have a nice day."

"You too," said Lu, sliding from the booth. "And you," she added, slipping past Dakota and his mother.

"Meat!" said Dakota.

"Bug!" Lu said.

The two women exited the restaurant and stood silently for a moment. Beatrix opened her automatic umbrella directly over her own head, not in the mood to share. Lu didn't care. The gray drizzle was cool and bracing, like the spray from a breaking wave.

Beatrix and Lu did not look at each other; they didn't have to. Each thought: *So we both have dark eyes, so what? I am not like her. And she is nothing like me. She will never understand how terrible it is, how much it really sucks, to have so much responsibility and so little control.*

"What were they babbling about in there?" Beatrix said finally.

"I think Heather used the word *gestalt*," said Lu.

"What does that mean?"

"Gestalt means—"

"*I* know what the word means, but what does it mean that *Heather* knows what it means?"

"The end of the world," said Lu.

What it did mean: They wouldn't be coming here again. Rage, hostility, jealousy, resentment—these things they could bear; people endured worse than that every day. They were not poor, not hungry, not plagued by plagues or flattened by natural disasters. They didn't have the energy, maturity, frontal lobotomy, or whatever else you needed for this first-wife-second-wife-Chinese-royalty crap, and they didn't know anyone who did. The old battles made so much more sense.

"Well," said Beatrix. "I guess that's it."

"Yep," said Lu. She watched Beatrix run to her car, the woman's heavy footsteps spraying stars all around her. Lu shivered under the buzzing baked potato long after Beatrix had gone, the rain picking at her hair, her face, her sudden, bitter grin. *Here I am,* Lu thought. *Julia Roberts, smiling bravely into the future with my big, big teeth.*

# THE BUNKO BUNNY

*I have no luck.* Glynn remembered this snippet of movie dialogue, but not the actress who said it or the name of the movie. She did recall a histrionic mass of corkscrew curls, a chewy New York accent, a tragedy: The husband she loved had been hit by a bus before they could have a baby. *No baby. No husband. No luck.*

Glynn figured it was better to have no luck than bad luck; even inertia was preferable to chaos. Glynn herself knew a lot about chaos because she had plenty of luck: a little good, some bad, all of it adding up to insanity. She had thermodynamic luck; the odds for explosion were high. Who cared that you shouldn't apply the laws of thermodynamics to human relations? She had atoms, she had energy. There must be, she decided, a scientific explanation, an underlying, imperceptible flame beneath her feet.

An example: Glynn wanted to play super couples bunko,

but George would have none of it. Here she was, ten minutes before everyone was supposed to show up, cross, sweaty, trying to convince him. Not that she could gather up all those husbands at the last minute, but still, there was the principle of the thing. One had to have principles. And anyway, he'd gone and devoured the box of spinach tarts that she thought she'd hidden underneath the frozen pizzas, and she'd been forced to run—literally—to get more.

"I'm not playing anything called 'super' or 'bunko,'" he said, his face washed out in the glare of the TV.

"But they're your friends," she said.

"They're your friends. They're my friends' *wives*."

That was the point, but Glynn didn't say it. Glynn was the new wife. The young one. But she wasn't so young. And George was her second husband. She was between jobs and, she hoped, between children. Anyway, she had to make a good showing, and she hadn't gotten remarried to go it alone.

And speaking of showing. "Will you please turn that horrible stuff off? You know how I hate it."

George tugged on his bottom lip. "Did you know that it only takes five pounds of pressure to rip a person's cheek away from the gums?"

"Ugh, George. I don't know why you feel the need to share these things with me."

George tore his eyes away from his new favorite program: *Autopsy!* "I love you."

She wiped the back of her hand across her brow. "We shouldn't have moved," she said, though the move was due to her own faulty logic, her luck. Their future seemed so ripe with possibility, why not move to a nice neighborhood in the suburbs, send Joey to a decent school for once, settle in, settle down? But that was before the budget cutbacks that cost Glynn her job, the strain to make the mortgage. Before she discovered that her new neighbor was a mortician and that her husband had never lost his little-boy obsession with all things torn and bloody. "We shouldn't have bought a house near those people."

"Who?"

Though she was irrationally fond of him—from his Muppet-oboe voice to his feline fits of ecstasy—she sometimes wondered if George was breathing through both nostrils. "You *know* who. The Addams Family."

"He said that if he gets a call for a body tonight, I can go."

"You're not serious."

"It's a necessary profession." George turned back to the screen. "You can't just leave a lot of dead people lying around. It's unsanitary."

The first time she'd brought George home to her mother's for dinner, his nerves had gotten the better of him and he'd ended up berating her mom and stepdad about their injudicious use of water. "You're watering the lawn *and* using the dishwasher. And the pool! Do you know how many gallons it takes to fill a pool?"

Her mother's verdict: "He'll need some encouragement, that one."


The bunko box waited on the dining room table. This was the box that jumped from hostess to hostess, a box that her ex-sister-in-law, Moira, had solemnly handed off to Glynn the week before. "This is it," she'd said in a tone that meant, to Glynn, *Don't fuck this up.*

Inside the box: dice, three for each table; scorecards; tiny little pencils; a large brass bell; and the bunko bunny, floppy eared and absurd in its polka-dotted boxer shorts. Joey would have gone nuts over the bunny, would have grabbed it and tortured it and then refused to give it up on pain of . . . well, on pain of pain. She supposed it was lucky—in the good and not thermodynamic way—that he was at his shithead father's for the night.

*At his father's,* she corrected herself. *Do not even* think *shithead.* Thinking led to speaking, and speaking led to parroting, and then there would be another infuriating letter from the shithead's attorney, *from his father's attorney,* about therapy and respect and the positive impact fathers have on the lives of their children. She'd said one little thing—one thing!—after the shithead had started dating that bitch. *Woman.* After Joey had come home from a visit and informed Glynn that his father, the positive influence, and the woman, the positive influence's influence, thought it was okeydokey to sleep in the same bed on a kid weekend and leave boxes of rubbers inadequately concealed for children to find. And bring home. And show to their still-prone-to-outbursts mothers. "Mommy? What's 'pleasure'?"

Glynn placed three dice on each table along with a scorecard and some pencils. She ripped open bags of M&M's and Reese's Pieces and poured them into the matching candy bowls they'd gotten as wedding presents, one per table, and then into some larger bowls at the bar. Indulging her librarian's lust, her secret craving for order, she arranged the liquor bottles alphabetically, lining them up in neat rows. Martinis. Check. Mimosas. Check. Manhattans. Check. Beer, wine, even a nasty bottle of candy-cane-flavored grain that some alcoholic neighbor had given her for Christmas. She could make any drink the wives could think to think of and a whole bunch they couldn't.

*Bring them on,* she thought. She was a wife, a wifey-wife, the wifey-est. *Look at these M&M's, will you?*

Of course, none of this was what she wanted to be doing on a shithead weekend. No, these weekends were their "young marrieds" weekends, where she and George could eat four-course breakfasts, see R-rated movies, or grope in the living room—things she hadn't been able to do freely for more than seven years. It was a pleasant—and unsettling—side effect of the shithead's visitation schedule. It hadn't started out that way. Those first sonless days after the separation, she had lurked and moped, a thin haunt in her own house, unmoored and outraged. After a while, though it seemed impossible, she got used to the days without her son, got used to herself without him. Now, when he was home, she began to crave the days he wasn't, that lazy sweep of hours in which she was relieved of monitoring the appetite, bladder, and emotional development of another human. And then he was gone again, and just folding his little underpants could make her weep. Split custody split her down the middle, until one day she was both mother and not-mother, two-faced like some goddess, but a crazy one, always turned the wrong way. And it made her despise her ex-husband that much more.

The doorbell rang. Glynn ran a finger across her teeth to ensure no lipstick had strayed there and watched George trundle upstairs, where he had promised to stay all evening. Then she opened the door.

"Is your doorbell broken or something?" said Moira, her hair blown straight enough to shear her blouse. "I've been standing here for ten minutes."

"Really?" said Glynn. "I'll have George look at it tomorrow."

"Sure, sure," Moira said, and threw her coat over the banister. "I need a drink. You wouldn't believe the week I've had." She marched into the living room, where Glynn had set up her bar, and sifted through the bottles. "Ryan is driving me crazy. I don't think he's spoken a civil word to me since he got back from that stupid fishing trip that Ben took him on. Now, he fishes. Since when does that rotten bastard fish? Do you have any Campari? I'm feeling Mediterranean today."

Campari. "I have everything else," Glynn said, surreptitiously pushing some bottles back in line.

Moira heaved one of her theatrical sighs. "What the hell. I'll have a Scotch and soda. The effect's the same." The doorbell rang, and Moira looked up, frowning. "Your bell works fine."

"I'll get that," Glynn said.

One by one, eleven women arrived, threw coats over the banister, and ran for the bar. As they plunged into the bowls of candy and poured themselves an assortment of drinks, Glynn collected the $10 ante from everyone. She knew them all by name, except for one, a woman so dull that her name refused to stick in the mind. This woman did not mix a drink or dive into the candies, she skulked around tugging on her crispy hair, doing something weird with her lips, sucking them in and out like gills. Glynn found it difficult not to stare. Joey would never have let her get away with a habit like that. As a mimic, he was merciless.

Moira sidled up to Glynn as she struggled to hang the coats on the lone coat tree in the foyer. "What's Lu doing here?"

"She's taking Rosemary's place tonight," Glynn said.

"Lu is."

"Yes." A coat, gray and shiny like sealskin, slithered to the floor. "What's the matter?"

"Lu's married to Ward."

Apparently, Glynn was supposed to understand the significance of this. "So?"

"So? Roxie's here. Roxie's ex is married to Ward's ex, Beatrix."

"Oh," Glynn said. She felt the prickle of sweat underneath her arms—the creep of chaos—as she tried to work out the relational tangle. "Is that a problem?"

Moira blinked at her. "What do you think?"

"Lu isn't married to Roxie's ex. She's married to the ex of an ex. What do they care? They probably don't even know each other, right?" she said, hoping that this once Moira might humor her. After Moira had divorced Tate, Glynn's brother, Moira had declared them the only extended family to have ever survived a divorce intact.

"Of course they know each other," Moira said. "The knee bone's connected to the hip bone by the thigh bone, you know?"

Campari and now anatomy. Glynn reminded herself that Ben, Moira's second husband, had walked out on her recently, and one had to be compassionate at times like these. "Sorry," Glynn said. "What?"

Moira pinched the bridge of her nose, like a teacher with

a particularly dense student. "When Little Miss Hot Pants finally moves in with your ex, Joey will find out all about her and tell you. You'll hear about her parents, her hobbies, the fact that she calls your ex 'Motor Hips' when she thinks Joey's not listening. And she'll know all about you, too, down to your bra size. That's what sucks about divorce. You can't keep a damn thing secret from anyone anymore. You know what I mean."

No more coats would fit on the rack. Glynn was left holding the slippery gray one, which she hugged as if it were a diary. "Well, I don't know what I can do about it."

"Nothing," Moira said, shrugging. "Now," she added. She threw back the dregs of her Scotch. Then she flexed a bicep and tested it with a finger.

Glynn wondered what kind of drink she should have, besides big.


Glynn had arranged three card tables in her family room, labeled "High," "Middle," and "Low." Glynn drew the head table and found herself sitting across from Roxie, while Moira took the "Middle" table with some of the other girls. Lu, Glynn noticed with relief, sat with the losers at the "Low" table.

Roxie declared herself the scorekeeper and rang the bell for the first round to begin. Even though Glynn had played before, even though the game was supposed to be mind-numbingly simple, she had to work to remember the few rules. In each round, players take the three dice and try to roll the same number as the round, called the target number. So in round one, you try to roll ones. Round two, twos. You get one point for each target number you roll. Three of a kind of any number *except* the target gets five points. Bunko is called when you roll three of the target number. Rolling bunko gets twenty-one points, but you have to yell it out to get credit. The round ends when the "High" table reaches twenty-one points.

"Rats," Roxie said after rolling, "not even one one." She slid the three dice over to Glynn.

Apart from the cartoon characters Joey liked to watch, Glynn didn't know anyone who could say "rats" and make it sound organic. Glynn rolled two ones, one one, and then bust. She watched Roxie scribble a "3" next to her name and tried to think of a topic that didn't have anything to do with Lu or the fact that Lu was married to the ex of an ex and might be privy to Roxie's personal information. Kids were safe. Except when they were on drugs. But Moira hadn't said anything about Roxie's daughter, Liv, being on drugs, just that she was a bitch. And that was all teenage girls, wasn't it?

"How's your daughter?" Glynn asked.

Roxie sighed, scratching her head with the end of her pencil. "Very skinny."

"In a good way?"

"In every way. Her body. Her outlook. Her worldview. I like to imagine she'll spend less time disappointed because of it."

Glynn handed the dice to a large, pie-faced woman named Sharon, who yelled, "Come on, baby!" before rolling three ones. "Bunko! Hey! I said bunko! Where's my bunny?"

Moira, who had been holding the bunko bunny, tossed it to Sharon, hitting her in her big head. "You're not supposed to get a bunko so fast!" Moira said. "I haven't even gotten a chance to roll yet."

"Me neither," said Rita, who was Sharon's partner but wouldn't get any credit for the bunko. Bunkos were an individual thing.

Sharon hugged the bunko bunny. "That's tough luck, ladies, this bunny's mine. And so's the pot tonight. I can feel it. It's my lucky night!"

"You always say that," said Rita, whose luck with bunko, a game that required absolutely no skill whatsoever, was as poor as her luck with men. Rita's bizarro husband, Mike, the Pyramid Scheme King, still fancied himself a jock, though his bandy legs had gone thick and his pectorals were as soft as breasts. At the last Super Bowl party, he'd tried to leap over one of the couches but caught his foot, fell, and knocked out his front teeth.

Glynn sipped her vodka-tonic, the lime juice stinging her lips. George might be a bit obsessed with death and dismemberment, but at least he had dignity; he had never injured himself trying to hurdle the furniture.

They played until the "High" table had twenty-one points. Roxie rang the bell to signal the beginning of round two and tucked the pencil behind her ear. "So, Glynn. How old's your son now? Five?"

"He's seven," said Glynn. "But sometimes he's two. And twenty."

Sharon threw the dice again. "My girl was born thirty, so I guess that she's now about forty-two. She's currently having her midlife crisis. She's not actually playing with her Barbies anymore, she just makes them have sex."

"I did that," Rita said.

"You had sex?" said Sharon. "That *is* news. What was it like?"

"Oh. I meant about the Barbies," Rita said.

"What about the sex?"

Rita pulled at the neck of her sweater. "We're trying to have another baby."

Sharon grunted. "Oh, *that* kind of sex."

Roxie turned back to Glynn. "Is your son with your ex-husband tonight?"

"Yes," Glynn said. "It's working out well." *Do not say shithead do not think shithead.* "Joey loves his father." A little sliver of lime had worked its way between her front teeth, and she worried it with her tongue. "Sometimes it's a little weird for me," she ventured. "To be without him. Joey, I mean." She wanted to say that it was also hard *with* him, harder than it had ever been before, but she couldn't bring herself to say it.

"You girls better stop yapping and roll," said Sharon. "Put down two for me, Roxie. I rolled a two and two."

Roxie wrote a "2" next to Sharon's name and grabbed the dice. One two. She passed the dice to Glynn, who got one two in each of eight rolls—eight points—before coming up empty.

"Isn't he living with someone now?" Roxie wanted to know.

"Who?" said Glynn.

"Your ex-husband."

*Bitch. Bitch, bitch, bitch.* "He has a girlfriend, but they're not living together."

"Yet," said Moira, who had tipped her chair back and was listening in.

"Um . . . bunko?" called a voice from the back, from the losers' table.

"Jesus!" Moira said. "Can't a girl get a chance to roll before someone else gets a bunko?"

Sharon tossed the bunko bunny over the "Middle" table to Lu, who promptly dropped it.

Roxie touched Glynn's hand. "Sorry," she said. "But you know, she could turn out to be a nice person."

Glynn felt suddenly sarcastic, and she didn't like it. "Oh, sure," she said. "Is *your* ex's wife nice?"

Roxie tapped the pencil against the table. "Well, we're not exactly typical. You wouldn't want to use us as an example."

Glynn wondered about the word *us*. Roxie and her ex? Roxie and her ex and his wife? The wife's ex? How big did "us" get?

There was a thud from upstairs, and everybody looked at the ceiling. Glynn closed her eyes, imagined her new husband leapfrogging over the furniture.

"What the hell was that?" Moira said.

"The cat," said Glynn. "Just the cat."

"You don't have a cat," Moira said.

Glynn swallowed the rest of her drink. "The dog, then."

They were on round six of the third game when someone rapped on the front door with the knocker. Moira, brandishing her third or fourth Scotch, said, "It's the cat!"

"Why don't you guys go to the kitchen and have some food? I've got spinach tarts keeping warm in the oven."

"Spinach," said Moira. "Who serves vegetables at a bunko

bash? We're here to get drunk and fat, aren't we? We want hypertension! Clogged arteries and dead brain cells!"

"The tarts have lots of cheese," Glynn said as she walked to the door. Because of her luck, she expected anyone and everyone—the cops, the firemen, the physics department of the local high school—everyone except her ex-husband's girlfriend, that is. But it *was* her ex's girlfriend, Stacey. So-proper-except-for-liking-to-leave-rubbers-around-to-advertise-her-sexual-peak Stacey, standing there in her skinny jeans, holding Glynn's son's hand.

"Glynn," Stacey said. She was as tall as a model, with perfect, even teeth. "I'm happy you're home."

"What?" Glynn said, looking toward the street for her ex-husband. "Where's Derek?"

"Out of town," Stacey said. "He was called away this afternoon. They had some sort of problem with the plant in North Carolina or South Carolina. One of the Carolinas." Stacey made spacey comments when she was uncomfortable; that's what Derek, Glynn's ex-husband, had said. "He took a two o'clock flight."

When Glynn was uncomfortable, she got anal and aggressive, which Derek had also pointed out. "Derek left this afternoon?" She looked at Joey, who was glaring at no one or nothing in particular. "What about Joey?"

"Yeah," said Joey. "What about me?"

Stacey's absurdly full lips quivered. "Derek said it was all right if I took Joey to dinner before dropping him off here."

"But why didn't he call me?" *Why didn't he warn me?* Glynn thought. But of course, that was ridiculous. Since when do you need to be warned that you have a son? You *al-*

*ways* have a son, don't you? When do you suddenly not have a son?

"He *did* call. He talked to your husband."

At this, Joey looked at his mother. "Dumb George."

Glynn closed her eyes and leaned against the doorjamb.

Stacey pulled herself up to her full height, her Armani glasses sliding down her nose. "Look, if you're busy, I can take Joey for the night—"

"No. No," Glynn said, horrified at the turn this conversation was taking. "Of course not."

"It's just that I have to work in the morning. New client. You know the drill."

If Glynn had had access to a drill . . . *Do not think about drills.* She took Joey by the shoulder and peeled him away from Stacey's side. "I can care for my own son."

Stacey's hands tightened around her shoulder bag. "I know," she said. "I was just saying . . ." She brushed away a lock of her hair, which was thick and wavy and perpetually windblown, like that of an actress at a photo shoot. Glynn could see that she was trying to be civil, and she felt a teeny bit sorry for her, an ass-impaired woman in her skinny pants. Yes, this was the person who had told Joey that his mother had "issues." Yes, this was the person who had told Joey that perhaps his mother was "a little too afraid of being replaced." Yes, this was the person who was ten years younger than Glynn, with better skin, better hair, and a better job. Glynn hated her guts, but she liked her feelings pure and unadulterated by pity. She wished Stacey would say something incendiary so that Glynn would have a good excuse to smack the fancy eyewear off her face and then keep smacking. Heat, entropy.

But Stacey, Glynn knew, was from somewhere out east where they jumped horses in their spare time, where they did not say incendiary things to their lover's ex-wives, except behind their backs.

"I guess that's all, then," Stacey said. "Derek should be back in time for Joey's Wednesday visit."

Glynn nodded. Stacey gazed down at the top of Joey's head. With her eyes, Glynn dared Stacey to try to touch him. But she didn't. She just turned around and walked away, her bony turkey back straight and tall.

After she had gotten into her car and driven off, Joey looked up at Glynn. "She says it's about time you got a job."

"Well, she's right about that," Glynn said, sitting on the stoop.

"I told her that you were my mom. That's your job."

Glynn smiled up at him. "And you're right about *that*."

Joey reached out to pluck some bright red berries off the bush crouching next to the door. "Are we going to be outside for a while?"

"For a while."

"It's kinda cold."

"Yeah, but you're a tough guy."

The tough guy nodded, shaking the berries like dice in his hands. "I'm going to smash these on the sidewalk."

Her question was pure reflex: "Why would you want to do that?"

"It will look like blood."

Sigh. "Of course it will."

• • •

It appeared that the girls had devoured the tarts and moved on to the contents of the freezer. The smell of tomato sauce spiced the air, and Glynn could see the frozen pizza boxes littering the countertop.

Moira staggered into view, framed by the decorative arch separating the front hallway from the kitchen. "Ho!" she said thickly, swaying as if she were a sailor just finding her sea legs. "What's the kid doing here?"

"He's just saying hi."

Glynn steered Joey into the living room and promised to give him a slice if he went upstairs and hung out with George. Quietly.

"I don't want to be quiet," Joey said. He spied the bunko bunny, which lay on its face on the floor by the losers' table. "What's that?"

"It's Moira's, and she'll be really mad if something bad happens to it, okay? Please go upstairs and be quiet. Mommy has some friends over."

"So?" he said loudly, thickly, swaying on his feet, like Moira in male, and in miniature. The woman whose name Glynn always forgot skipped into the living room, a bouquet of gnawed pizza crusts in her hand, stopping abruptly when she saw Glynn and Joey standing there.

Joey snickered. "What's that lady doing with her face?"

Glynn took him by the arm before he had the chance to either get a chokehold on the bunko bunny or do another of his wicked impressions and brought him upstairs to the bedroom, where George was playing video games. When she'd married him—her George, lover of nonlinear foreign films and discordant, arty jazz—she hadn't figured on the video

games. The explosions and the blood and the bodies bursting like firecrackers.

"Hi, Joey," George said. To Glynn, he said, "I thought he
was at his dad's."

"He was. What's-her-face dropped him off because Derek
got called out of town. She said he spoke to you about it."

"Derek did call, I forgot to tell you. But I'm sure he didn't
say anything about anyone going out of town."

Glynn was equally sure that he had, but she didn't want to
get into an argument about it. George did the best he could,
she knew he did, but he still hadn't quite grasped the fact that
Joey wasn't a housecat with his own kitty door to the yard.

Joey staggered around drunkenly, rolling his eyes back in
his head. "What are you doing?" George said.

"Moira," said Glynn. "Look, the girls are still here, so
could you keep an eye on him for a while?"

"Sure," he said. "How long's a while?"

"I don't know. A while."

"Can I play Mortal Kombat, Mom?" Joey said.

George put the console on the bed. "Can I take him with
me if I go out?"

"Go out where?"

"You know," said George. "The Addams Family?"

"Who's that?" Joey said.

"No! You guys just stay up here. You're not even supposed to be home, remember?"

"Phone home," Joey said, and held up his finger. "Can I
call Dad?"

"What?" Glynn said, more sharply than she wanted to.
"Why?"

"Because he's my dad. Children should always be able to

call their fathers whenever they need to," Joey said, his voice prim, sounding much like a certain assless person.

*Do not say shithead do not think shithead.* "I didn't say you couldn't call your dad. Of course you can. But he's out of town right now."

"So I'll call the town he's in."

"You know, I think I am in the mood for a little Mortal Kombat," said George, relenting. "You can be that chick with all the arms, if you want."

Glynn gazed out the window, watching the trees buckle under a sudden wind. Joey had always been a somewhat moody and stubborn child, but all the changes in his life had turned him cranky and mulish. Glynn had read all the books, knew the stats, understood that in the long run, boys fared much better in remarried families, in the company of other boys. Joey seemed to tolerate George well enough, and vice versa. But their common interests were the bloody sort—the war games, the crime dramas, the nature specials that began with some sweet animal baby sticking its innocent nose out into the world and ended with some bedraggledlooking predator making a snack out of said baby. When she protested, they called her a girl, which made her furious, because she was beginning to suspect that gender had something to do with it all. Why couldn't she just get along with Stacey? her ex wanted to know. *He* certainly didn't have any problems with George.

Ha. That was because her ex was more successful than George, or thought he was. And because, while Joey thought George was okay, he clung to his father like a kinkajou to a banana. These things vindicated the ex in every mind but Glynn's.

Besides, she "got along" with Stacey just fine. They

managed. Glynn didn't appreciate the snide little comments and judgments delivered via her son, that's all. She
didn't care for the preferences and desires and observations
of this strange woman creeping into her life, this spacey-
Stacey-seepage.

And she didn't like the woman's stupid, beautiful face.

When you got right down to it, this was all her ex's fault
for trying to turn his girlfriend into his son's mother, for as-
suming that if there was a lunch to be made, then his woman
would make it; a nose to be wiped, then his woman would
wipe it. Glynn knew her ex would be content with a little
hero worship and the ability to retreat to the drawing room
when there was some child-made mess to clean up—part of
the reason she'd left the bloodless asshole in the first place.
It wouldn't be long before Stacey or some other Stepford
Girlfriend was helping with homework, taking an afternoon
off to cart Joey to the dentist, or staying home with him if
he was sick. When would Stacey start believing that she had
a right to an opinion? When would she tell Joey to call her
Momma-Two or Stacey-Mommy or some other such horror?
What if he *wanted* to? What if he could sense his own
mother's distraction and sought comfort from the other
woman trying to win his favor? What if he turned into one
of those wretched men who were always seeking comfort
from some other woman?

Glynn shuddered, suddenly frantic. She'd have to draw
the line somewhere, but where to draw it? The Little League
games, the parent-teacher conferences, something.

The ringing phone banished thoughts of pelting Stacey
with baseballs and chalk-choked erasers. George snapped up

the receiver with one hand while still punching buttons on
the game console with the other.

"Yeah, speaking," he said. "Yeah." He glanced at Glynn,
then at Joey. "No, we're not doing anything, either. I'll be
by in five minutes. I'll bring Joey."

"George," Glynn said, her voice a warning.

"Relax," George said after he'd hung up. "Stiller's wife left
him with the kids. We're just going out for a little ice cream."

"Ice cream?"

"Ice cream," George said firmly.

"Hey!" yelled someone from downstairs, Moira. "Someone
die up there or what?"


Entropy measures the tendency of energy to disperse, to dif-
fuse, to become less concentrated in one place or one energetic
state. But entropy, sometimes called time's arrow, moves, com-
fortingly, in a logical direction, something that could be antic-
ipated, something that could be understood. Rocks don't roll
uphill of their own volition. Water doesn't freeze without im-
petus. Kettles don't suddenly heat up by themselves.

Glynn watched her husband and her son slip out the front
door, tearing off one of her fingernails with her teeth, con-
sidering the physical laws that governed her personal universe: people shooting every which way, bouncing off one
another, and spinning out on unknown trajectories. *Ice cream,*
she told herself. *He said they were just going out for ice cream.*
She had to start trusting them sometime, hadn't she? Otherwise, where would her husband and son end up launching
themselves?

The girls had rearranged themselves in her absence, the

winners moving to the head table and the losers to the losers' table. They'd played several rounds, someone rolling for
Glynn, and Glynn and Moira had come up winners. Now
Roxie and Lu sat across from each other at the winners' table.
Both blanched with embarrassment when Moira said: "Hey,
you guys are practically related! It's like some sick game of
six degrees of separation or something!" After that, they
played a few more games in relative silence, until Moira got
bored and grabbed the dice.

"Come on, fours!" Moira yelled, the word *fours* sounding
like *force*. One four. One four. Two fours. She rolled three
sixes—five points there—then nothing. "Damn it," she
grumbled. She tossed the dice to Roxie, who tried to catch
them with one hand and missed.

As Roxie plucked the dice out of the carpet, Lu said, "I
meant to tell you, Glynn. There are some openings at my
agency. That is, if you're still looking for a job."

Roxie rolled a four. "I thought you worked for a real estate agency."

"I do," Lu said.

"Oh," Glynn said, looking from one woman to another. "I
didn't know real estate agencies need librarians."

Moira slapped a palm on the table. "Everybody needs
librarians."

"They don't need a librarian. They need an office manager." Lu took the dice from Roxie. "I'm sorry. I thought you
just wanted something to do during the day, when your son's
at school."

"She needs a job, not a little something to do," said
Moira, slurring. "Some of us have to work for our bunko
antes, you know?"

"Sorry," Lu said. "I just thought . . . sorry."

"No," said Glynn. "Thanks for letting me know."

Lu shook the dice in her hand. As there had been a bunko drought since she'd gotten hers, she'd brought the bunko bunny with her, propping the thing on the table. Before each roll, she eyed it warily, as if it might suddenly begin leaping about.

Roxie swallowed visibly. "So, Lu. What's your husband up to these days?"

"He's in Virginia," Lu said, blowing her bangs off her forehead. "Then Tennessee, then Georgia."

"Does he have to go?"

Lu frowned. "Sure he has to go; it's for work. . . . Crap. I'm busted. Here—" She thrust the dice at Glynn.

"So you're a single girl this month?" Roxie asked.

Lu snorted. "I've got Devin full-time. I'll have the other boys this weekend, because their mom is going out of town."

"It must not be easy for you, Lu," Roxie said. "With the boys. Stepfamilies can be so complicated."

"You think?" said Lu. She was pretty, but in a hard way. She had a U-shaped line forming underneath her nose, possibly from sneering too much.

"I don't know. Joey's doing all right with George," Glynn offered.

"Ward's kids are okay. Mostly, anyway," Lu said. She met Roxie's eyes. "Their mother's another story."

"Oh, I'm sure she's trying," Glynn said.

"Yeah, well, she could try a little harder."

Glynn threw the dice, sending one careening off the table. "Heh," she said. "I guess I don't know my own strength."

Roxie leaned back in her chair. "Kids aren't easy whether they're your own or someone else's. Believe me, I know."

"Yes," Lu said, her face softening, the little U-shaped line smoothing out. "Of course you're right."

"We all just have to do our best," Roxie added.

Lu put her elbows on the table, her expression suddenly open. "But then, that's the thing, isn't it? Everyone is doing something different, and everyone thinks whatever they're doing is best."

Another loud bang, the front door flying open, whacking against the wall. The girls swung their heads toward the noise in unison, like a herd of prey animals at the crack of a branch.

"Mom! Mom!" Joey shouted, running into the living room. "I saw a dead guy!"

"Was it my ex-husband? Please say it was my ex-husband!" Moira said, nearly tumbling out of her seat. Her eyes found Roxie. "You date Tate. You date my ex! How could you?"

Roxie laughed, got up, and helped Moira back into her chair. "You were the one who set me up with your ex. How could *you?*"

Glynn looked at George, who was standing in the hallway, half-sheepish, half-irritated. He'd probably told Joey to keep it a secret, not knowing, not understanding that Joey would be too excited to keep his mouth shut, that children don't have the willpower for mystery.

"He was hit by a bus! But he wasn't all smushed up or anything."

Glynn sighed. Really, after all the death they'd witnessed on TV, was it so bad that her husband and son had gone out to see an actual dead person? Death was an inevitable part of life, wasn't it? Part of the cycle of things.

Then again, maybe the vodka-tonic had addled her brains. She should have fought harder, that was her problem. So many things seemed inevitable to her, had the hypnotic perfume of fate about them, that she was beaten before she even began, like the one lame antelope on the plain.

"Why didn't he look smushed, Mom?"

"I don't know, Joey. Sometimes people don't look smushed even when they should look smushed."

"Mr. Stiller is going to drain all his blood into a bucket. That's what George said. Right, George? They hang the guy from hooks."

The woman whose name Glynn always forgot gasped in horror and sucked on her lips so hard that they disappeared into her face.

With her son and husband and all the girls watching, Glynn rested her forehead against the cool table. There was no controlling this, her luck. She would have to let Joey go a little; she was already doing it. Through her, Joey and George were united in all their gross and glorious boyness; through Joey, she and her ex-husband were locked together forever in their awkward, stupid dance. And if Derek married Stacey . . . well, her stupid-beautiful face would be everywhere. And they'd all expect Glynn to make room at the parent-teacher conferences. The Communions. The weddings. The baby showers. Joey's relationships would become something else, something outside of Glynn's reach, as prodigious as that reach—the reach of mothers—was. And wasn't she herself moving out of her own reach? Becoming some other woman, married to some other man, possibly, soon, mother to some other person. Dispersing. Spiraling outward into the world, both more and less than before.

*Fine. Fine,* she thought. *But not now, not yet.* Didn't she deserve some stillness? Some silky vacuum into which she might slip, secure in the fact that no rocks would ever roll uphill and nothing would ever change?

With the girls still watching—gaping—Glynn lifted her head and scooped up the dice, rolling idly at first and then with more purpose. She rolled again and again, until she got what she wanted. Three fours. Bunko. "Take the box," she said, telling them, telling them all. "Take the booze. Take the candy. Take whatever you want. The bunny's mine."

# THE DOG NEXT DOOR

Tate's sister is calling about her latest obsession: family therapy. Ever since her ex-husband announced that he was getting remarried, Glynn calls to ponder aloud which school of thought might be best, which members of the family should attend, which issues should be explored (as if the pre-dominant issue isn't Glynn's hatred of her ex's wife-to-be).

"Glynn," Tate says, sneaking a glance at Roxie, who's scratching at her bare foot in a distracted way, "can we talk some other time?"

"I was just thinking that all of this is connected some-how."

Tate sighs. "All of what is connected?"

"To our parents. They're divorced and divorced again. Then I got divorced."

"But you are married now," he reminds her. "To a great guy."

His sister is not to be stopped. "And you're not only divorced, you date bimbos. Don't deny it, Tate. *Bimbos.* Well, except for Roxie. I like her. Anyway, don't you think all these things are connected? Shouldn't we explore these connections so that our children don't suffer the way we did?"

At the moment, the only connection Tate wants to make is the naked kind, the only suffering in his pants—which are, disappointingly, still on his body. Roxie's knee begins to bob up and down, and he knows he can't keep her waiting; Roxie is perpetual motion personified. Thirty seconds longer and Roxie's knees will bob her right out the door.

"Glynn, I have to go, okay? We'll talk when I come get the kids. Or at the beach house this weekend." *Or never. The twelfth of never. How's that look for you?*

"I didn't call to talk about therapy. Your son bit Joey, that's why I called."

Tate squeezes his eyes shut. "Boys hit each other."

"*Bit.* As in *bite.* As in *teeth,*" Glynn says. "This has really got to stop. You shouldn't be begging me to watch your kids when you're supposed to be spending time with them. You shouldn't be on a date right now. Ryan shouldn't be biting people. There's a problem here. *You* have a problem."

Another glance at Roxie. "I hear you, Glynn. Really. And I promise we'll discuss it later."

There's silence on the line, then: "Fine." Before she hangs up, she adds, "Don't do anything I wouldn't do."

Ten minutes later, he's cupping Roxie's pointed elfin chin in one hand and using his other to trace her clavicles. Roxie has delicious clavicles, one slightly lower than the other. He rubs the thin skin between them as if making a wish. For a moment, he almost wishes that she could come with him to the beach house. Roxie would look amazing in a bathing suit. Marilyn Monroe, all soft skin and dimpled elbows.

"The dog's watching," Roxie-Marilyn says, pulling away from him.

At first he thinks it's one of those off-kilter Roxie jokes, the kind that don't make much sense but are sort of funny because she won't stop making them. He doesn't have a dog. He smiles and leans in to kiss her.

"Really, Tate, the dog's watching. That dog next door." She gestures to the basement window, where a rectangular vent is open in the center of the glass blocks.

And there he is. Small, white, wiry haired. Black nose, black eyes, gnashing teeth bared. For once, he isn't barking. He's too busy staring. And breathing weird panty dog breaths.

"Great. A doggie voyeur." Tate shrugs and inches closer to Roxie. "Ignore him."

"I can't." Roxie looks at her watch. "Besides, I have to go."

He wants to stamp his foot like a child. "Why? It's only nine."

"Liv's out with her new boyfriend. I don't want them to come home to an empty house."

Tate gets it but pretends he doesn't. "And?"

Roxie smooths her hair and tugs at the hem of her blouse. "Tate, you have a teenage daughter. You know what I'm saying. I don't really need to make it so easy for them to hook up, do I?"

Tate doesn't tell Roxie that the top two buttons of her blouse are unbuttoned, because he's still hoping that he might unbutton the blouse all the way. He reaches out and curls his arm around her waist. "Hooking up sounds like an excellent idea." Actually, it's the whole idea, the reason he brought Roxie into the basement in the first place. It's cool down here, and dark, and the red couch is the pullout kind.

Roxie submits to a few minutes more of kissing, sighs in his ear when he puts a hand on her breast, but then pulls away again. "Sorry, Tate. I can't relax with that dog staring at me. And I really do have to go." She gets up from the couch and gathers her purse and shoes. "You're not mad, are you?"

"No," he says, though he's exasperated. Roxie is sexy but flighty, too often running off to her bitchy daughter, or to the university library, or to her "job" as a counselor on a suicide hot line. And if she isn't running off, she's questioning her role in the universe and the meaning of life and the meaning of meaning so much that he gets too annoyed and distracted to pull out the couch.

Next time, he thinks, he'll pull out the couch first.

But he sees those lovely clavicles peeking out of the top of her shirt and gives it one last try. He presses his lips to the base of her neck, sliding his fingers around her rib cage.

"I won't be seeing you for a week," he says.

"Whose fault is that?"

"My dad's. He's the one who wanted the trip."

Tate sees that Roxie wants to say, You could have asked me to come with you, or, I've never met your parents. But she doesn't. She's given up on such things. Instead, she says: "Can't blame Daddy for your whole life." She squirms in his Pepe LePew arms, trying to get free.

•    •    •

The trip from O'Hare Airport to Surf City, New Jersey, which should have taken a grand total of five hours—including the flight and the drive to the beach—takes twelve instead, due to storms, crew problems, and strong winds (which Tate hears as "strong whims"). Tate spends the whole flight trapped next to a crazy man, who, between loud air phone calls, rocks in his seat, weeps, and prays in a mystery language. Toward the end of the flight, the attendant barks at Tate for having his tray table down when he wasn't supposed to. "Okay," Tate mutters like a teenager, "that's fair."

"Where have you been?" his father wants to know when Tate and the kids drag themselves into the house at nine P.M. Tate's father is deeply tanned, but his normally silver hair seems thinner, whiter. He's holding a glass of clear amber liquid.

"Where do you think we've been?" Tate says, setting the suitcases on the floor. There are at least four hundred suitcases.

"If I knew where you've been," says Tate's father, "I wouldn't ask. What happened?"

Tate grunts. "Various natural and unnatural disasters," he says. "Strong whims."

Ryan slumps into the nearest chair. "Daddy had to sit next to a crazy guy. And then they made him put his table up."

"Who?" says Tate's father. "What table? The crazy man's table?"

"Never mind," Tate says. "It doesn't matter. We're here now."

"Thank God," says Ashleigh, kissing her grandfather's cheek. "I need a drink."

Tate's father starts. "Excuse me?"

"Kidding, Grandpa," Ashleigh says. "Cool house."

Technically, the house belongs to Renee, his father's wife, who inherited it from her parents. It's a modern affair, gray and boxy and enormous, with decks on all three floors and a fourth on the roof. With his drink, Tate's father points out the high ceilings, Italian tile floors, open staircases, private outdoor shower, Jacuzzi.

"So, how are you doing, Dad?" Tate says after every architectural detail has been duly noted and appreciated.

His dad takes a sip of his drink, and Tate sees that his hands are shaking and his eyes are bloodshot. "How does it look like I'm doing?" his father says.

*Well, Dad, it sort of looks like you've been smoking crack for a day or ten.* But Tate won't say it; he'll leave the interventions to Glynn. "You look fine," he says.

His dad holds out one quaking hand and smacks Tate's cheek lightly. "That's it," he says. "We're all fine, aren't we?"

Like the house, Renee—Tate's "stepmother"—is also a modern affair. After the tour of the beach house, she appears from nowhere, sweeping down the steps in a champagne-colored pajamalike outfit. The only thing missing are the jewel-studded mules; Renee's feet are bare, the toenails painted a bright pink. There's a thin silver ring around the second toe of her right foot.

Tate nods a greeting. "Say hello to your grandma Renee," he tells Ryan, nudging him toward her. She hates to be called "Grandma." She's only forty-nine, just four years older than Tate, and takes great pride in the fact that most people think she's at least a decade younger.

"Call me Renee," she says for the thousandth time, giving Tate one of Renee's patented Looks of Doom and Destruction. Tate rather enjoys Renee's patented Looks of Doom and Destruction and does what he can to keep them coming. Renee detonated his parents' marriage in nuclear fashion some twenty-nine years before, and Tate has never forgotten it, or quite forgiven it. Payback, bitch, and all that.

"Where's Glynn?" Tate says.

"She's not getting here till tomorrow morning," Tate's father answers, sounding relieved. Tate himself is relieved. He'd had enough of his sister a few nights ago, when he went to pick up his kids after his date with Roxie. Glynn threw open her door and began berating him as soon as he stepped onto the porch. She said that Ashleigh was too old for a baby-sitter, that this was the second time Ryan had bitten Joey, that all of this was related to their parents and possibly their parents' parents—their grandfather had divorced their grandmother back in the 1950s. It was about time, Glynn announced, that they saw a family therapist to work it all out, connect the dots. There were so many, many dots. Dots upon dots.

Tate stood there trying to connect the dots, trying to remember the first time Ryan had bitten Joey. He had a dim memory of someone crying, but that could have been anything. Someone was always crying somewhere. "I don't remember Ryan biting Joey before," he said, then followed her into the house.

"Of course you don't," Glynn said. She lowered her voice to a whisper so that the kids, wherever they were, wouldn't hear it. "You weren't there, you idiot. You were out on a date with that woman, What's-her-name. The one with the boobs."

"Actual boobs? Crazy."

"And now he's bitten Joey twice. When I told him to leave Joey alone, he called me a jerk."

"I'll talk to him," Tate said.

Glynn put her hands on her hips. "What are you doing? You date all these girls, rattle around in that huge house, and you dump your kids whenever and wherever. These kids need you, Tate. Especially now that Moira's not with Ben anymore."

Ben. Right. Überdad. Superstep. Not so superüber after all, since he cut out. But then, Tate didn't have much to say on that score, since he'd cut out once, too. He felt a small abrasion of guilt, and then more guilt because he didn't feel guilty enough. He could never feel guilty enough. But then the kids were fine, mostly. Mostly, they were fine.

Glynn didn't think anything was fine. Glynn talked and talked and talked: "They're totally lost. And what did Ashleigh do to her hair?"

After Moira told Ashleigh that she couldn't dye her hair colors not found in nature anymore, Ashleigh had dumped a bottle of peroxide on her head. Now her hair was a peculiar shade of orangey blond usually seen only in servings of sherbet.

"It's better than the pink," Tate said.

"I liked the pink," Glynn said. "That was interesting. This is frightening."

"That's her job," Tate said, "to frighten her parents."

Glynn snorted. "She hasn't frightened you yet. But she will."

• • •

Renee doesn't look frightened as much as irritated by Ashleigh's sherbet hair, cutoff shorts, and sloppy tank top that displays the straps of her navy blue bra. "Let me show you to your room," Renee says. "You and your brother will be staying downstairs, right by the—"

"What?" says Ashleigh. "I'm not sharing a room with *him*. Let him and my dad share a room."

"Ashleigh," Tate says.

"What?"

Tate raises a significant eyebrow at her, a gesture that seemed to hold some power when his ex-wife did it. Ashleigh raises her own brow, probably because she's seen her mother do the same thing. "You never said anything about sharing rooms," she says.

"You thought we'd rent you your own hotel suite?"

"Why not? You're a doctor. You can afford it."

Though she seems to be enjoying the exchange, Renee steps in. "You can stand your brother for a few nights, Ashleigh, I'm sure. Follow me. Bring your suitcases. And don't drag them. I don't want any scratches on the tile. It cost my parents a fortune to fly it in from Milan."

"I'm not staying in a room with him," Ashleigh announces.

"Well, then," Renee says, "I'm sure you'll be very comfortable sleeping on the driveway."

She sweeps out of the room and down the hall, Ryan and then, after a few minutes, Ashleigh waddling haphazardly behind her like gormless ducklings.

Tate's dad laughs. "Renee always had a way with children."

•   •   •

In the morning, Renee makes blueberry crepes with fresh whipped cream.

"Ryan doesn't eat blueberries," Tate tells her. "He doesn't like fresh whipped cream."

Renee dusts sugar over a plate. "Everyone eats blueberries," she says.

"Ryan doesn't."

Renee looks at Tate. "Everyone does."


At the beach, Tate buys Ryan a hot dog with mustard, which Ryan then feeds to the seagulls.

"I'm not buying you anything else, then," says Tate. "I don't care how hungry you get."

Ryan says, "I don't like blueberries."

The lifeguards watch as Ashleigh peels off her jeans and T-shirt. Underneath, she is wearing a red bikini with letters scrawled across the ass.

"What's that on your butt?" Tate says, too loudly.

"Everything she wears has something on the butt," Ryan says.

"What are you talking about?" says Ashleigh, twisting to see. "Oh, that. It says, *Dump Him.*"

Tate sticks his feet in the sand so that the tops don't get burned. "Who's 'him'?"

Ashleigh shrugs. "All of them." She sees the lifeguards and waves.

•   •   •

Tate wakes from a nap. He hasn't been to the beach in years and remembers now how much he likes it—the crash of the waves, the fresh skin smell of the sea, the sand scratching at his toes. He switches from the blanket to a beach chair and takes in the scene. Ashleigh is talking to the lifeguards, looking up at them with one hand tented over her eyes, one arm folded underneath her breasts. Ryan builds an elaborate sand castle high up on the beach—so that the water won't rush in and wreck it, he told his father. The water always wrecks it.

And then he sees her, the girl. She's not his type—too small, too tanned, and way too young—but he can't help staring. Years ago, when Tate was an intern, he'd walked into an examination room and seen this girl, this luscious, juicy-looking girl, perched on the table, and he'd thought, *Whoa.* He'd immediately fought to gather himself, to cover his feelings with that expression of professional dispassion he'd believed he'd perfected, but it was too late. The girl had seen the look on his face, the look of whoa, and wasn't sure how to react to it. She'd seemed both pleased and alarmed at the same time.

The effect he has on most women, now that he's thinking about it.

This girl, small and tanned and way too young, flips to her stomach. She sees him watching. She glances quickly behind her, to make sure it's her he's admiring, then undoes the back of her lime bikini top, exposing her smooth back and the whitish sides of her breasts. She smiles as she presses her face against the towel.

She doesn't look the least bit alarmed.

•   •   •

Glynn and his nephew, Joey, are at the beach house when Tate and the kids return from the ocean.

"Where's your husband?" Tate says.

"Oh, don't remind me," says Glynn.

"George had to go to Africa," Joey offers.

"Alabama," Glynn says.

Joey shrugs. Africa, Alabama, same difference.

"What's in Alabama?" Ashleigh pronounces "Alabama" the way other people say "Antarctica."

"Not us," Glynn says. "It's a good thing, too, because there aren't any beaches there." She eyes Ryan. "And there won't be any biting *here,* will there?" When Ryan doesn't respond, when he lifts his sandy boogie board and strokes it like a dog, Glynn pinches her brother.

"Ryan," Tate says. "No biting, all right?"

Ryan rolls his eyes and mumbles, which Tate takes as a "yes." It's enough for Joey, who immediately asks to borrow Ryan's boogie board when they go to the beach the next day.

Glynn pinches Tate again.

"What?" says Tate.

"I've almost got Mom talked into family therapy."

"No, you don't," Tate says.

"Yes, I do."

"No, you don't. She told me when I last talked to her that she'd go to family therapy when they pry her gun from her cold, dead hands."

"I think it would help us all understand this legacy," Glynn says.

"Please tell me that 'legacy' means someone old and wealthy kicked and left us all a billion dollars."

"The legacy of divorce."

"The legacy of divorce is the legacy of divorce," Tate intones.

"That's exactly it."

"I know, you've told me. Over and over and over. And if you already know it, why do we need to go to a therapist?"

"We're not normal people, Tate. It's pretty clear to me that we're not normal people. The evidence is all around us." She flaps her hand at the screen door that opens out onto one of the numerous decks. Their father sleeps on a lounge chair, an empty glass on the table next to him. "We call a man who isn't our dad 'Dad.'"

"Glynn," he says, "he raised us."

"I know," Glynn says. "But it's not normal. I'm tired of explaining it. 'My dad, who's technically my stepfather but not really, because he's not married to my mom anymore, but he's still my dad, because he adopted me when I was five. No, I don't see my real dad, who isn't my dad anymore, because the other one is.' Who else has to say those kinds of things? Who else has to live like that? It's insane."

"You don't have to explain it to anyone, you know," says Tate. "You could just call Dad 'Dad' and leave out all the details."

"But they're important. Our pasts help to make us what we are."

*Our fats help to make what we fart.* "I know you're upset that Derek is marrying Stacey, but you'll get over it. I promise."

"Stacey has lips bigger than my whole head. In case of an emergency landing, you could use Stacey's lips as flotation devices."

"You will get over it," Tate says firmly. "And if you want,

you could buy flotation lips, too. Ask Renee where to get some."

Glynn wrings her hands the way Ashleigh used to when she was a baby and wanted someone to pick her up. "Derek invited me to the wedding. They're getting married at some estate on Lake Michigan. All the guests have to wear white for some insane reason. I'll look like a barge. A big white ex-barge."

"You don't have to go," he says.

"I have to go. You know I do."

"Okay. Do you want me to prescribe something for you?"

Glynn glares at him. "What are you implying?"

Renee stalks into the room, holding two small towels with tassels on the edges. "These are decorative towels," she announces.

Everyone turns to look at her.

"There are stacks and stacks of towels in the linen closet. I don't want anyone using the decorative towels anymore."

Ashleigh picks at her fingernails. "Why not?"

"Because," Renee says, eyes widening, "they're *decorative.*"

"Why did you hang them in the bathroom if you don't want anyone to use them?" says Ryan, looking up from his boogie board.

Renee stares. "Is that sand all over the floor?"

Ryan stares back. "We're at the *beach.* Beaches have *sand.*"

Tate's mother calls his cell phone just as he's finished lathering up with sunscreen.

"So," she says, "how is it? A castle on the edge of the ocean?"

"It's on the bay side, actually. A few blocks from the beach."

"Really?" Tate's mother says. "Slumming, are they?"

"Slumming with Italian tile," Tate tells her.

"Ah," she says. "Are you allowed to walk on it?"

"Sometimes. But Renee does like to follow everyone around with the broom."

"Renee with a broom! I can't believe it! She might get blisters on her delicate fingers! She might ruin her manicure!"

"There are emergency numbers on the fridge just in case," Tate says. "Plus, I am a medical professional, you know."

"Hmm," his mother says. "How are the kids? Are they having a good time?"

"The boys are fighting over the boogie board, and Ashleigh is flirting with the lifeguards. They torment Renee by kicking sand around the place and refusing to eat her food."

"So they are having fun," she says.

"I think so."

"Are you?"

"Glynn won't come to the beach because she's worried about melanoma. And she keeps talking about family therapy."

"Oh, God! That girl! She always did read too many books. I told her that she should have been a lawyer. No, she wanted to be a librarian."

"She's just upset about Derek getting married again," Tate says.

"Well," says his mother, "I can understand that. But instead of therapy she ought to think about beheading all the roses in the garden. That's what I did on the day your father married Renee."

"Therapeutic."

"Speaking of therapy, how's your father's drinking?"

"Let's not talk about that, Mom. Let's talk about something else. How's Len?" Len is his mother's third husband. The first, Tate's "real" father, she refers to as her "practice husband." The second, Tate's adoptive father, she refers to as "that bastard." Or sometimes "schmuckface." "Putz-a-doodle-do."

"Len," his mother says. "Len is Len."

"What's he up to these days?"

"Who?"

"*Len,* Mom."

"Oh. Let's see. He found a three-headed ant on eBay, and he's been bidding on it for the last twelve hours. We're up to fifty-six dollars. For an ant."

Tate takes a deep breath, filling up his cheeks and exhaling like a balloon. "Okay. How are you?"

"How do you think I am? My children are off at Renee's fantasy castle by the sea, and I'm here with *Len.*"

A flash of lime green catches Tate's eye. The girl's back, spreading out her rainbow-striped towel. She sees Tate and smiles.

"I keep looking for Mr. Darcy and all I find are a bunch of Mr. Collinses," his mother says. "Jane Austen has completely ruined marriage for any woman born after 1800. Someone ought to have arrested her for suggesting that men have inner lives, that men have something in the center.

There's nothing but nougat in there. No fudge, no caramel."
She laughs, delighted by her own analogy. "And you can forget about nuts."

There's another girl with her, this one in pink. Green
nudges Pink with a tanned toe, and Pink begins to giggle.

"I don't mean you, Tate. When am I going to meet this
woman you're dating? What's her name? Trixie? Was her
mother a truck stop waitress, by any chance?"

Green hooks a finger into the top of her bathing suit and
flashes a nipple.

"Tate?" says his mother. "Hello, Tate?"


For dinner, Renee makes softshell crabs with wild rice.
Ryan says they look like giant bugs in piles of dirt. Joey sees
what's for supper and starts to cry.


After the meal, or rather, after the tantrums, Tate loads
Ryan, Joey, and Ashleigh into the car and drives to the nearest ice-cream shop, Scoopy Doo. Ryan demands the biggest
banana split—four scoops of ice cream, two bananas, three
types of sauce.

"You wouldn't need such a big ice cream if you had eaten
your food," Tate says.

Ryan's expression says his father has gone crazy if he ex-
pects a boy to eat giant bugs in dirt piles. Joey shyly asks for
a Super Scoopy sundae.

Ashleigh doesn't want ice cream. She wants to talk.
While the boys chase each other around the parking lot, she
asks to live with Tate. "Mom doesn't understand me."

Tate is momentarily speechless. Then he says: "I don't understand you, either."

"Yes," she says, "but it's okay if you don't understand me. You're not supposed to."

"I'm not?"

"No, you're my father. You're supposed to misunderstand everything. You're supposed to hate my boyfriends. You're supposed to threaten to shoot them or cut them into little pieces or something."

He does not want to talk about this. "Speaking of boyfriends, how's Kevin?"

"Devin. With a D. And you're not listening! You're supposed to hate my clothes and disapprove of my choices."

"What choices are we talking about here?"

"My *choices*," she says again.

He thinks of his house, where he has only the barest essentials: a couch, a chair, a coffee table, a plasma TV. After the divorce, his ex, Moira, kept the house and Tate moved into his own. He doesn't know why he bought a house; he never liked the upkeep a house required, never kept up with upkeep. But Moira said it might be a good idea that the kids have their own rooms in his place, and he thought it was a good idea, and everyone he talked to said, "Oh, what a good idea." But the kids had slept in those rooms only a handful of times, and they never really decorated them. And sometimes, after he's had a glass of red wine or two or three, he can admit to himself that it was a bad idea to buy a big house, a bad idea to buy any kind of house. Why does he need a house? He doesn't need a house. Every woman he brings there says the same thing: "This could use a woman's touch." And they're right, of course, women are often right about a lot of things, but he doesn't want a woman's touch. At least, not that kind of touch. They should feel free to touch *other* things, though, the women. Sometimes, if it's the right woman, he says as much.

Roxie hasn't said anything about a "woman's touch." He likes that about her. She doesn't seem to notice the mess, the lack of decoration, the Ramada Inn–ness of his whole enterprise. Plus, there's her name. That strange throwback of a name. It makes him feel young, it makes him feel he's living in an Elvis movie or maybe a dream.

But sometimes he feels Roxie staring at him when she thinks he isn't looking, sizing him up, and he wonders when she will start pushing, asking him if their relationship is "going somewhere." It seems to Tate that all women think they should be going somewhere. Tate wants to know where all the women think they are going.

"So can I live with you?" Ashleigh tosses the sherbet hair from her shoulder. "I really want to get my belly button pierced."

Glynn finally decides to come to the beach. She wears a large floppy hat, a bathing suit with a skirt, and a white film of SPF 10,000. She opens up a book, but Tate knows she's not going to read it. She blurts, "What do you remember about our father? The real one, I mean."

"What do I remember about him?" Tate doesn't remember much and doesn't care to remember. Why would he want to remember anything about a man who walked out on him and his sister and then kept walking? But his sister is looking at him as if she's dying of thirst. "Uh . . . he was tall.

And he had a lot of hair all over the place, like a crazy man. He had crazy man's hair."

"Crazy man's hair. I must have inherited that. What else?"

"He collected stamps. I remember him hunched over those books, pasting the stamps into them. He tried to get me interested, but I didn't care about that stuff."

"Did he play with you?"

Tate shrugs. "He taught me to ride my bike. What do you remember about him? Anything?"

Glynn folds the page in her book. "Not much. I know that he was a smoker."

"What?" says Tate. "No, he wasn't."

"Sure he was," Glynn says. "You don't remember those skinny cigars? They stank up the room."

"I have no idea what you're talking about."

"We used to fight over who got to blow out the match, so he'd always light two matches, one for each of us."

Tate shakes his head at his sister. "You must be thinking of someone else. He wasn't a smoker."

"Yes, he was."

"Glynn," he says, getting a little annoyed, "I don't think he smoked a day in his life."

"You just don't remember, that's all," Glynn says.

"*You* don't remember," Tate says. "You were three years old."

Glynn opens her book, closing the subject.

"Why did you ask me what I remember if you don't want to know what I remember?" he says, though she continues to ignore him.

Tate pushes his sunglasses up the bridge of his nose in disgust and pretends to sleep. But he can't stay irritated for long; the sea air scours away irritation, exasperation, consternation. Anyway, he has something else to think about. Green is no longer wearing green, she wears a new bathing suit, a polka-dotted one. Though it covers more of her body, she seems more naked in it, as its different shape reveals secret stripes of untanned skin.

Tate's not-father father insists on taking the family out for dinner, despite the fact that his wife has planned to make lobster tails with drawn butter, despite the fact that his wife is furious. "I can't understand what we're doing here," she says, yanking her napkin off her plate in disgust and spreading it over her lap. Tate notices that when Renee frowns, she develops jowls. When he was little, he always wished that people looked more the way they really were inside. Renee's jowls say a lot. Renee's jowls say, *I will devour your soul if you let me. I will stuff you with bugs and dirt.*

"The kids didn't want lobster tails," says Tate's dad. "Kids don't eat that sort of thing."

Renee doesn't care what kids eat. "What am I going to do with all that lobster?"

His father's expression is blank when he says, "Maybe you can give it to one of your friends."

"Which friend?" Renee says. "Who are you talking about?"

"I don't know any of their names. Isn't that funny that I don't know any of their names? You'd think I would by now."

Renee studies her husband. "You've been drinking again."

"No more than usual."

It seems the kind of drama that teenagers live for, but Ashleigh isn't interested. "So, Dad, have you thought about what I said?"

"About what?" says Tate.

"About living with you."

Glynn dribbles clam chowder down her chin and neck. Ryan's head snaps up. "Are we moving in with Dad?"

Tate says, "I don't think that's the best idea."

"Why not? We can hang out together. Do things, like we used to."

What things? All Ashleigh ever talks about is her hair or her nails or her boyfriends, and sometimes, sometimes, he has to remind himself that he's her father. He doesn't feel old enough to be Ashleigh's father—or Ryan's, for that matter. When did he have these children? How long ago could it have been? His forty-fifth birthday had come as a huge surprise. He does not want any more surprises.

"Well?" Ashleigh says.

"I'll think about it."

"I know what that means," says Ryan. "That means no." He wraps his hands around his warm Sprite. "Don't put ice in it," he told the waitress. Ryan hates ice, hates that the ice could abruptly avalanche as he's drinking and hit him in the face.

Glynn carefully crumbles crackers into her soup. "How about a compromise?"

"What do you mean?" says Ashleigh.

"Maybe you could spend part of the week at your dad's and part with your mom," Glynn says.

Ashleigh considers this. "That could be okay. As long as the weekends are with Dad. Maybe like Mondays, Tuesdays, and Wednesdays are Mom's or something. Or just Mondays and Tuesdays."

Glynn nods energetically. "Yes, like that. I'm sure if you sat down with your parents and discussed it, you could work it all out." She glances at Tate. "I don't know if your father has mentioned it to you, but we're thinking of taking the whole family to therapy. This is just the kind of thing that you could work through there. I think that it will be good for all of us to hear what you have to say."

Tate wants to throw something at her.


Tate has now seen both of Green's nipples and one butt cheek. He can't imagine where she'll go from here. Will she strip on the beach? Stride naked into the sea foam like Aphrodite in reverse? Behind dark shades, he watches, every muscle in his body tensing in anticipation.

"Stop staring, Dad."

"What?" He sees Ryan, Joey behind him, both wearing little boots of wet sand.

"You keep staring at those people," Ryan says, dumping his boogie board on the blanket. "It makes you look weird."

"I'm not staring," Tate says. "And I don't look weird."

Ryan grabs a towel and, with it, wraps his head like a turban. "You always look weird."

Tate considers his son. "This from a boy in a turban."

"Not from me. Ashleigh." He points to the lifeguard stand, where Ashleigh chats with two boys who look as if they've been sculpted entirely out of toffee. "She told me to tell you that the girl is too young." Ryan puts his hands on his hips. "Are you going to marry her?"

"No, Ryan. Ashleigh's got the wrong idea. I'm not marrying anyone."

"My dad's getting married," says Joey. "Mom doesn't like it."

"Do you blame her?" Tate says.

"Huh?"

"I mean, are you sad that your dad is getting married?"

"No," says Joey. "Mom got married, so it's only fair that Dad gets to. That's what I keep saying, 'It's only fair, Mom.' It just makes her madder."

"Yes," says Tate, glancing at the girl in green. "Women are like that."


Ashleigh is talking. Something about a lifeguard, and dinner, and a party afterward.

"So?" she says. "Can I go?"

"Right now?"

"No, next year," she says. "Yes, now! Dominic is off duty at five and wants to take me to this restaurant he knows."

Tate eyes the lifeguard. Instinctively, he sucks in his stomach, then, feeling foolish, releases it. "Which restaurant?"

"How do I know? And who cares?"

Tate waves his hand. "Fine, fine," he says. "Just tell Dominic the lifeguard that he needs to have you back at the beach house by eleven. Do you know the address?"

Ashleigh recites the address and the house phone number. "Okay?" she says.

"Okay. Just keep your cell phone on."

She yanks some shorts out of a canvas bag and steps into them, one foot, the other foot. "You're not going to, like, call me in the middle of my party, are you?"

"I will if you're late."

Ashleigh rolls her eyes, her gaze settling on the girl in the lime bikini. "You should probably go back to the beach house now. Renee will probably make you some snail-slime salad or whatever."

Tate plays it casual, doesn't look at the girl on her rainbow towel. "I'll go in a bit. I like the beach in the late afternoon," he says.

Ashleigh's lip curls. "Yeah," she says. "I bet."

He sends the boys back to the water for one last swim and settles back into the sand chair. Except for Green and for Tate, the beach is empty. It's safe for whatever might happen to happen. The girl in the green bikini is smiling, smiling, smiling, and untying her bikini top, and he will get another glimpse of something secret and delicious from a girl who isn't alarmed, who isn't looking to go anywhere. Except there's something blocking his view, some boy in his way, some blond boy in blue swim trunks, who is not just blocking his way but is walking toward the girl in the lime bikini, dropping to his knees on the rainbow-striped towel, and grabbing the girl around the waist. They fall to the towel, giggling. The boy pulls an orange blanket over them, the lime bikini top tossed out onto the sand, where it curls like seaweed. There is frantic, frenzied motion under the blanket. The moans carry in the wind.

*This is a family beach,* Tate thinks. *A family* beach!

His cell phone saves him. He fishes it out of the canvas bag. "Hello?"

"Hey, you," Roxie says. "How's the beach?"

"Fine," says Tate. *We're all fine.* Lime green bikini bottoms fly out from under the blanket.

"You sound a little funny. Are you coming down with a cold?"

"No, no," he says. More firmly, "No."

"That's good. Are you guys having fun?"

The orange blanket moves rhythmically. "Yeah," Tate says. "We're having a great time." He realizes that he is no longer a man, he is a dog. A voyeur dog, the dog next door. He adds, "Wish you were here."

"Really?" says Roxie. "Too bad you didn't ask me to come."

"I should have," he says.

She's silent for a moment. "Yeah, you should have. But you didn't."

"Next time I will."

"What are you saying?" she says.

He turns away from the undulating blanket, from the ocean. He doesn't know what he's saying. He's not saying anything. What is there to say? He doesn't want to marry Roxie. He doesn't want her to meet his extended family, the high-maintenance, emotionally crippled parade. He likes things the way they are, Roxie in one corner of his life and everyone else in the other. Doesn't he? Isn't that what he likes?

"Tate?" She sighs then. "Tate, look. Don't worry."

"What do you mean?"

"Don't worry about me getting too serious."

"I wasn't—"

"Yeah, you were. I'm not stupid, Tate."

"I never said you were," he says stupidly.

"If it makes you feel any better," she says, "I have a date tomorrow night."

"You what?"

"I have another date. I figured you wouldn't mind. I figured you'd be relieved." Her laughter sounds fuzzy in the cell phone. "You *are* relieved."

Relieved? "Uh, I—"

"I finally get it, Tate. I get that this is a casual thing for you. And you know what? I'm okay with that. I'm not ready for anything serious anyway. I already have one failed marriage under my belt, I'm not looking for another one. I'm really not."

"Oh," he says. All he can think to say. He risks a glance. The orange blanket is still. *That was quick,* Tate thinks nastily.

"Well, I didn't expect to be talking about this today, but I'm glad we did," Roxie says. "Liv is here, so I should go. But I'll try to call you tomorrow."

"Right," says Tate. "Have fun on your date."

There's a pause, and then: "Geez, Tate."

"Geez yourself," he says. "Bye."

"Tate . . . I . . . Okay. Bye."

He flicks the phone shut and tosses it back into the canvas bag. Then he takes off the sunglasses and throws them into the bag. If he'd had anything else to throw, he would have thrown that, too.

When he finally looks up again, the girl is back in her lime green bikini, a huge grin stretched across her face. The blond boy nods, shouts, "Like the show, old man?"

It's one A.M., and Ashleigh still isn't answering her phone. Glynn wants to know why Tate would allow Ashleigh to go out with some strange boy in the first place.

"First you tell me she's too old, and now you're telling me she's too young," Tate says.

"Too old for a baby-sitter, too young to be out with marauding strangers, yes."

"Marauding? What do you mean, *marauding?*"

"Isn't that what you're worried about? Isn't that why you're upset she's not home?"

Tate's father, still up, still swirling amber liquid in a glass, grins at him. "I seem to remember worrying about the same thing when you'd go out."

"Not now, Dad," says Tate.

"What? A man can't worry about his son?" He booms the word *son.* As a matter of fact, he's always boomed the word *son,* as if it were never a sure thing.

"Dad?"

"Yes?"

What comes out of Tate's mouth is not what he'd intended to say. "Do you know . . . do you have any idea if my father, the biological one, was ever a smoker?" He does not look at Glynn when he says this.

"I think he was. Why?"

Tate licks his lips and notices that they are raw and sore, burned in the sun. "No reason. I just don't remember him smoking, that's all. I . . ." He trails off. There's something about this, the not remembering, that is bothering him, but he doesn't know what. Why doesn't he know?

"Your mother was sure it would turn you and Glynn into human smokestacks. Bad early influence and all that. Speaking of your mother, how is she?"

"Don't worry about Mom," says Tate. "You have other things to worry about."

"Like what?"

"Your drinking."

"Not you too!"

"Okay, then. Your wife," Tate says, punching in Ashleigh's number again.

"My wife," says Tate's father. "Yes. She can be worrisome. Or she was. Now I just don't care anymore."

"Dad, I'd love to talk to you about Renee, but I'm trying to find Ashleigh right now."

Tate's dad grunts. "She'll come home when she's ready."

"What if something's wrong? What if that moronic life-guard kidnapped her or attacked her?" He's sure to say "moronic" and not "marauding."

"I'm sure she's fine. She's just trying to scare you."

"Why would she need to scare me? Why does everyone keep saying that?"

"Who's everyone?"

Glynn's face is so full of worry, so full of genuine concern and real feeling, that it hurts to look at her. "Forget it," Tate says. "I'm going out to look for her."

"It's not going to help," his father says in that same booming voice, echoing throughout the house. "The time you should have paid attention is over, don't you know that?"

But Tate is already out the door, already down the street. Instinct takes him the few blocks down to the beach. As he walks toward the water, grit fills his shoes and abrades his skin. There are couples dotting the sand, murmuring in the dark. He has no idea if she's here, if he'll be able to find her. He moves from couple to couple, dot to dot, looking for her sherbety hair. He's about to start shouting her name when he sees the X marking the spot: Ashleigh, spread-eagled on the wet sand, the tides licking her toes. He runs over to her, an awkward, broken lope.

"Ashleigh," he says, shaking her shoulder.

"What?" she says groggily. She frowns. "Dad? Where's Dominic?"

"I don't know," Tate says. "What are you doing? Are you drunk?"

She pushes his arm away and sits up. "Get off."

The stink of pot and alcohol mix with the tang of the sea. Her clothes and hair are mussed, disheveled. Anger boils in the pit of his stomach. He didn't think she could be this reckless, this dumb. "It's past one in the morning. Where the hell have you been? What the hell have you been doing?"

"Oh, chill out, Dad," she says. "We were here, like, the whole time." She scans the beach. "Where did Dom go?"

"I told you to be home by eleven."

She's not even looking at him, she's pulling her cell phone from her pocket, she's trying to focus on the screen. "How many times did you call me? . . . God. There's like sixteen missed calls."

He grips her arm again. "Ashleigh, I asked you a question. What have you been doing? Were you smoking? Drinking? Did you lose consciousness?"

"I was just resting my eyes."

"And he just left you here? You have no idea what he or anyone else could have done to you," Tate says.

"I know what he did to me." She yawns. "I'm so tired. I want to go to bed. Is the house far? I hope you brought the car with you, 'cause I don't feel like walking."

"Ashleigh," he says, "Ashleigh," as if the sound of her own name might clear her head. "Do you have any idea how dangerous this is?"

"What?" She struggles to her feet. "The tide, you mean? I would have moved out of the way." She laughs. "Anyway, this isn't a big deal. Dom's just a little summer fling."

He stands, too, searching her face. She's perfectly serious, she's perfectly oblivious. That's what does it, the obliviousness, the blindness, the unbelievable stupidity and self-absorption, that's the thing. He thinks: *We should go to family therapy. That's what we should do. Shouldn't we?*

He grabs her cell phone from her hand and launches it into the ocean. "You're grounded."

She rounds on him, incredulous. "You can't ground me."

"Yes, I can." By the elbow, he yanks her across the beach. Several couples unlock lips to watch.

"Let go of me," Ashleigh says. "Let go!"

"No."

"You don't even care about me! You don't care about anyone! What are you doing? Why are you doing this?"

He doesn't answer. He knows a thing or two about therapy, knows about acting as if. A caring man would yank his daughter across the sand. A caring man would ground her. A caring man would put a stop to all of this, right here, right now.

Tate makes like a caring man and drags his wayward, shrieking daughter back to the castle by the sea, where her family waits.

# HUG MACHINE

He was a junior capitalist, Lu knew that much. He liked
to frame himself in doorways, forearms braced in the jambs
shoulder level, hands hanging open and relaxed, broad
cheeks and wide-set eyes hinting at Slavic ancestry. *Kama
Sutra* scenarios looped relentlessly through her dirty mind,
scenarios impossible for so many reasons: Lu was married, he
was engaged, Lu was head-butting forty, he was all of
twenty-whatever, and Jesus, who could braid themselves like
slipknots without pulling something, anyway? Lust, she
thought, was ridiculous, and even more ridiculous in middle
age, more oral, more aggressive, an absurd flashback to
babyhood. When she looked at him, her mouth watered,
every golden inch of this boy a place to sink her teeth.

"I like it," he said. "But I don't love it."

"It" being the tenth condo she'd shown him in three
weekends. How he could pull off a new condo before a big

wedding, Lu didn't know, but he seemed confident—an investment, he'd told her. He'd live in it himself for the eighteen months of the engagement, and then he and the wifey—a little slip of a thing Lu had met only once—would buy a house and rent out the apartment. That was the plan: Buy up property, rent it out. He wanted lots and lots of property, didn't believe the rumors of an impending real estate collapse, or perhaps believed he'd outrun it. Sometimes he took stairs and sidewalks at an easy jog, turning back to look at her as if she were the one with the ball and she need only toss it to him and he'd win the game for everyone.

"The lake view is obscured by that other building," he said, "and that bathroom. What were they thinking?"

"It's brand new," Lu said. "New fixtures, tile, tub."

"The tub is orange. Who ever heard of an orange tub? Looks like a baby aspirin explosion."

She realized that he had paused, waiting for her to respond, only after she'd been staring at his belt buckle for a long, delicious half minute. If she yanked on it, he'd peel away from the door hips first. "It's bad," Lu said, collecting herself, "but not the worst. You should have seen some of the places I've been in. Ducks everywhere."

He blinked at her with eyes the color of the Blue Grotto. "Ducks? Like real ducks?"

"No, I mean country decorating. Duck borders. Duck wallpaper. Ducks carved into the banisters." She'd never been in a place where there were ducks carved into the banisters, but what do you say to eyes like that, with them blinking at you? A stacked deck if there ever was one.

He hung his head, then glanced up out of the corners of his Grotto-blues. "Sounds pretty nasty."

"Nasty is right," she said, feeling the flush bloom on her cheeks. *God, Lu, get a grip!*

He smirked one of his little smirks, private and sweet, one that had most likely been wielding power and influence over every female he'd encountered since the sixth grade. "So, where to now?"

"Um . . ." She looked at her clipboard, though she knew exactly what was written there. "There's a new listing over on Farwell. Neighborhood's a bit dicey, but it's up-and-coming." She flushed again. There. He'd reduced her to middle school. All she needed were the pimples and the high bullet breasts, and the transformation would be complete. "But unfortunately we can't look at it today because the owners are having some work done."

"Oh," he said. He dropped his arms from the wall and slipped his hands in his pockets. "How about next Saturday?"

"I won't be available to show you around next Saturday. Family event. My husband's family." She rolled her eyes and made a waving gesture, a "you know about husbands and their crazy events" gesture, except that he probably didn't, being that he wasn't even a husband yet, and why was she rolling her eyes at the mention of her own husband?

"So the Saturday after next?" His blond hair was fine, baby's hair. Lu wondered if a lover had ever shampooed it for him, if he was old enough to have had someone in his life he called "lover."

"If you really want to see it next Saturday," said Lu, "I can make arrangements for another agent to show you."

The smirk fell away, and he shook his leonine head, a single drop of sweat glistening in the chiseled channel over his lip. "No. I want *you* to show me."

• • •

"I bet you were doing that thing, too," said her sister, Annika, later, when Lu met her for drinks by her pool. "That preening thing where you toss back your hair and show your neck. You used to do that in high school."

"I did not show people my neck in high school."

"Yes, you did. You must have a thing about birds. That's how birds mate."

"I don't know what you're talking about. And I'm not mating."

"What would you call it?"

"Flirting."

"You don't know how to flirt. That's why you went around showing people your neck." Annika took a sip of low-cal sangria that they'd made from a Weight Watchers recipe. "Listen to that beautiful sound. You know what that is? The sound of naptime."

Asleep, Annika's triplets looked like a band of angels. Awake, they were tumblers from the Cirque du Soleil, only more talkative. "Aren't they a little old to take naps?"

"Who's too old for a nap?"

"That's true."

Annika pointed a finger. "I hope you're not tempted to do anything stupid."

"Of course I'm tempted. The Virgin Mary would be tempted. You would be." The jeweled drop of sweat had thrown her, that and the sudden loss of high school cool. Lu assumed that this lust was her own private experience, but what if it wasn't? The reciprocity, even the possibility, unnerved her.

Sex reduced, sex plundered, sex mauled, and it massacred—just look at what people would do to do it, what it did to people who did it. Lu used a spoon to dig out some of the fruit at the bottom of the sangria pitcher, secretly eyeing Annika's body. But the black bathing suit hid the cesarean scar and stretch marks Annika complained about so much, and the spider veins weren't as obvious as Annie said they were. Even the few extra pounds she carried gave her an attractive kind of plushness, lush goddess curves. *I guess it wouldn't be so bad,* thought Lu. *Would it?*

Annika lifted her sunglasses and peered under them. "Will you stop staring at all my figure flaws, please?"

"What flaws?"

"You can't fool me," said Annika, stretching, smiling. "You know you're checking out the damage." She flipped on her side and pointed behind her. "Look! I have mommy butt!"

"Your butt is totally the same." It wasn't, but it was still a butt to envy.

"I'll take your word for it." Annika sank back into the lounge chair. "If you're going to do it, you gotta do it now, honey. You're thirty-nine."

"So you keep reminding me."

"Your eggs have wrinkles."

"I earned every one of them."

"The rates of mental retardation and autism increase as a mother gets older."

"La la la. I can't hear you."

"You'll be close to sixty when your kid goes to college."

"Oh, for God's sake."

"I'm just laying out the facts."

"You want facts? The fact is that every time I think about having a baby, one of Ward's kids does something odious or perplexing, and then I get all confused. This has been happening for years, and I don't know what to do about it."

"Devin is graduating now, right? In three months he'll be off to college. So that's at least one less deterrent to procreation."

"True."

"Look at you. You're not even thinking about having a kid, you're thinking about doing a kid."

Lu popped a cherry into her mouth, plucking the stem from between her teeth. "He's not that much younger."

"Just ten or fifteen years." She stirred her drink. "I've got some wrinkle cream if you want it. What's his name, anyway?"

"Mr. Tasty Pants."

"Uh-huh. And what about the Happy Husband?"

"Ward's fabulous. He's marvelous. Nothing wrong with Ward."

"Okay, then. What's wrong with you?"


Lu turned the corner and ran, the same route she'd been running since she'd quit smoking—for good this time. *Nothing's wrong,* Lu told herself silently. Nothing serious, life threatening, or soul scorching, anyway. Even marrying into Ward's tribe had proven less traumatic than it looked from the outside, mostly, sort of, at least relative to her own chaotic youth that included stints as stepdaughter, half-sister, and loony tune. But she'd beaten it, done better, at least a little. They'd muddled through the drama of the first years of blended family life and had reached some sort of stasis: The boys achieved the ability to reason, the ex was down to only periodic fits of idiocy, and Lu had gotten used to living in a one-and-a-half-bath Chicago bungalow the size of an Easy-Bake oven. One adapts, one adjusts, life settles like a handful of feathers tossed to the wind—scattered but restful. So why would she want to stir everything up again with a baby, a helpless baby, an autistic, head-banging baby born of her old and shriveled eggs? Where was the wisdom in that?

She turned up the volume on her radio, picked up the pace. She'd heard somewhere that musical choices were pretty much set in stone by the time you hit age thirty-five, but Lu was determined to stay open-minded even on this small level. The pop station blared some rock-rap hybrid whose hook was *"Shut up! Shuuuuut up!"* She remembered the first time she'd yelled at the kids—well, not the kids, but *the* kid, Britt, the mouthy one. They were in the car on the way home from another tense meal in which Ward had tried to force Devin to eat something more substantial than a few crackers, Ollie bursting into tears when Ward scolded him for offering to eat Devin's food for him. Britt, who had the unenviable job of blowing off steam for the rest of them, cataloged a litany of random complaints on the way home, from his stupid fricking teachers to his stupid fricking mother to the stupid fricking window that was fricking broken and couldn't they just fricking *fix* it already? And Lu felt the heat rising from her rumbling belly, in which her cheese-laden meal was already padding a fifteen-pound weight gain that would take her thirteen months to lose, and she turned around and screamed, *"Shut up!"* to Britt, who was so surprised that he actually did.

So many ways to count progress.

Anyway, after all that drama, maybe it was regular old five-year itch that filled her head with obscenities about this golden boy, that set her hands to twitching whenever she saw a plump vein rising on the surface of his forearm. The late thirties sexual peak, the perimenopause her mother insisted was right outside the door, if not actually in the house.

Out of the corner of her eye, she saw a hulking black Ford Explorer inching up behind her. Her stomach did a little dance of apprehension the way it had ever since she'd turned twelve and realized the world was full of people with questionable intentions. She turned her head slightly just in time to observe the purple missile propelled in her direction, just in time to jump back. The water balloon exploded at her feet, missing her by a yard.

She whipped the headphones from her ears and watched as the Explorer drove away, the boys inside it screaming with high school hilarity. Forgetting that people had questionable intentions, forgetting that she was thirty-nine years old, a woman, and alone, she screamed, "You missed, you stupid morons! You little shits *missed* me!"

The truck shrieked to a halt in the middle of the next block, and Lu's heart leapt up and cowered in her throat. Would they get out of the car? Would they beat her up? Kidnap her for kicks? They idled there a moment, the truck's engine rumbling like some great, dark animal loosed from the deepest caves. Then the driver stepped on the gas, and the truck disappeared in a cloud of exhaust.

•    •    •

"Hmmm . . . ," said the man, inspecting some molding in the front room, trying to look as though he knew what he was doing. "Hmmm . . ."

The man wasn't thrilled with the house, Lu could tell. And though she couldn't really blame him—the house was a squat little wreck crouched on a stamp-size swatch of brown grass—she blamed him nonetheless, because he was making her work harder than she wanted to and because she would rather be sashaying around modest condos, Mr. Tasty Pants in tow.

The woman sucked on her own lips nervously. "Well, honey? What do you think?"

"Hmmm . . ."

Lu gave up and sat on the couch. For the life of her, she could not remember their names, kept thinking of them, insultingly, as Mr. and Mrs. Mister. What was worse was that she knew the woman, had seen her at one of Glynn's stupid bunko parties, parties she attended only out of a wish for more company, or rather, company more like Lu herself—a few fellow anthropologists trying to blend in with someone else's family, trying to dissect and understand its particular culture, trying to shape and influence without inciting the tribe to riot.

In this case, it had been explained to Lu in the car, the tribe had been left at home. "They don't want to move," the woman said. "Neither of them, though Dawn isn't making as big a deal of it as I thought she would."

"Are you kidding?" the man said. "Every time I come downstairs for breakfast she's shooting daggers at me. That kid has some attitude." *Ah, the stepfather,* Lu thought.

The woman blinked as if she had just gotten a faceful of cobweb. "She's been better lately."

"Come on."

"She has! She took out the garbage this morning!"

Mr. Mister turned around to look at his wife in the backseat. "You always defend her."

In the rearview mirror, Lu could see Mrs. Mister's cheeks growing red and hivey. "And you always defend Sloane. She's not perfect, you know."

Lu turned the corner carefully, hand over hand. *Stepmother.*

The man was cool. "I never said she was perfect."

"You act like it," the woman said, her voice cracking. "You always yell at Dawn more."

"Give me a break," said the man, turning to face forward again.

The woman crossed her arms and glared out the window for the rest of the trip.

Now, in the squat wreck of the house she knew they'd never buy, Lu wondered how this family could possibly function split down the middle the way it was. What were the odds of divorce in a second marriage? Sixty percent? Eighty? One thousand?

"I'm sorry," said the man, standing up straight. "I don't think this is going to work for us."

"Right," Lu said. "Let's move on, shall we?"

Vamoose the Wonder Dog—Moose for short—bonked Lu's legs with his nose as if he were some sort of living metronome while Lu chopped vegetables for a salad. Moose, they discovered soon upon adopting him, loved tomatoes, cherry being a particular favorite. He tucked the tomatoes into his cheeks like a squirrel and toted them around for a while before finally settling somewhere to bite down.

Lu dropped a cherry tomato to the floor, where it was soon sucked into the corgi's mobile lips, sticking out like a tumor. "You're a strange dog, Moose," she told him. The dog did not appear too concerned about this. He gave her leg another nudge and sprawled out in a sunspot.

The back door flew open and Devin ambled in. "Hey," he said to Lu. He stooped to pat the dog. "What's up, Moose Man?" The dog's tail thumped, but he didn't bother to stand. He was like that. His name, Vamoose, was born of the fact that the dog was the polar opposite of the term, ever present and everywhere, always underfoot. When they presented the dog to Ward, Ward took one look and said, "This dog thinks it's all about him." Lu had replied, "Well, it is, isn't it?"

"How was your last day?" Lu asked Devin.

"Boring," said Devin. "Hours of saying good-bye to teachers you didn't like in the first place."

Lu grabbed a carrot and peeled it, shooting orange ribbons into the salad and onto the counter. "You never have to go to that school again. Can you even believe it?"

Devin scratched Moose's belly, and the dog did a yoga stretch in response. "Yes and no," he said. "It's weird. Like, I don't know."

Lately, Devin had been trying something new: conversation. So far, he wasn't so great at it, and Lu wasn't at all used to it, but it was an improvement over the era that Lu now referred to as the Grunting Years.

"Yeah," Lu said. "It is weird. You want to leave a place for

just about ever, and then, when you can, you're not sure if
you're ready to go." She plucked a stray string of carrot from
the countertop, trying to think of what else to say.

"Here's something that should cheer you up," Devin said,
somehow understanding that she needed cheering. "I broke
up with Ashleigh."

"You did? Really?"

Devin smirked. "Don't look so sad."

"Sorry," Lu said. "What happened?"

"She was getting on my nerves. Acting all weird and shit.
Uh, sorry. I mean, and *stuff*."

"It's okay. I've heard worse. How was she acting weird?"

He shrugged. "I don't know. She just was. And it was getting old, you know?" Devin sat cross-legged on the floor and
ruffled Vamoose's ears. "I told her that since I'm going to
college in a few months, I didn't want to be tied down to one
girl or whatever. I want to have fun this summer."

"Really," said Lu. "How many girls do you plan on having fun with?"

"Ha, ha," Devin said, looking up at Lu out of the corners
of his eyes. "Hundreds, probably."

"How did she take that news?"

"What do you think?" Devin said, disarming her completely with a rare grin. "She was *weird* about it."

Lu nodded. "A lot of people are weird." The way Devin
sat made his long, gangly limbs look smaller, and she could
see the sweet, glossy curls on the top of his head. Without
thinking, she added, "Everything's weird."

"What do you mean?"

Lu hadn't expected the question and scrambled for an
appropriate answer. "Well, you're an adult now, right?

Having fun with hundreds of girls. Going off to college. Reminds me how old I am. Except I don't feel old. I feel the same as I did when I was a kid. Like you. I feel young. See? Weird."

"You're not that old," Devin told her, scratching the dog under the chin. "It's not like you're fifty or something."

She didn't say that fifty sounded pretty youthful to her these days. "True. It's not like I'm fifty."

Devin kept going. "And except for the ones under your eyes, you hardly have any wrinkles."

"Gee, thanks, Dev," she said far more forcefully than she intended, almost a shout. "I guess it's time for the Botox."

Britt appeared in the doorway. "Time for the Clorox?"

"We're all looking a little dingy," Lu said. She watched Devin for signs of annoyance, but he continued to pet the dog as if she'd never raised her voice.

Her saucy middle stepson sprawled in a kitchen chair. "So. What are we talking about?"

There was a brief silence before Devin said, "We were talking about you. We were wondering how many weeks it's been since you've been thrown out of class or off a team or something. We're thinking of calling the doctor. We're thinking of having it classified as a true miracle."

"Really?" said Britt, trilling the "r." "I think it's a miracle that none of my teachers or coaches are assholes this year."

"Britt," said Lu.

"I'm just expressing myself."

"But Ollie's not even here to correct you. Where's the fun?"

"Ollie doesn't care anymore," Britt said. He was wearing

his hair longish and shaggy now, like a yearbook picture from the 1970s. He loved to make phone calls with Lu in earshot, just so that she could hear him say: "You're the girl of my dreams, and I want my future to include you." If Lu hadn't known him, if he wasn't only sixteen, she might have believed he'd gotten permanent makeup tattooed on his eyelids and lips. He was that pretty.

"Haven't you noticed, Lu," Britt added, "that Ollie's too into his Game Boy to tell on me? I'm beginning to think he doesn't love me anymore."

"News, bro," said Devin. "Nobody does."

"That's cold," Britt said, teeth flashing.

"Cold but true," Devin said. "You've got a face only a stepmother could love."

"You sure? I wonder what Ashleigh would say if I called her. I think she's hot for me."

"She's hot for herself," said Devin. "Then again, so are you. Maybe you're the perfect couple."

Britt balled up a napkin and threw it. "Are we having dinner sometime this century?"

"No," said Lu. "Why would we do that? Besides, you have to go pick up Ollie at school."

"What?"

"You promised," said Lu.

"Why would anyone want to join the chess club, anyway?"

Lu shrugged. "Maybe he's looking to get thrown out of it."

"You know, you were always too smart for your own good." Britt pulled a banana from the fruit basket and his keys from his pocket. "I'll be back with the little darling in a few minutes. Don't eat real food without me." With the banana, he saluted his brother, Lu. Then he was out the back door.

Devin stood up, and the dog put on his wounded face. "I'm going to go call Shoop. See if he wants to go to a movie later."

"Devin," Lu said.

He turned. "Yeah?"

"Sorry about before."

"Huh?" he said.

"About raising my voice. The crack about the Botox?"

"Oh, that. Whatever." He fished a string of carrot from the salad and popped it into his mouth. At Lu's feet, Moose's eyeballs rolled back in their sockets like a shark's. Then he bit down into his cherry tomato, splashing the juice on Lu's feet.

She wanted to say: Thank you for talking to me. Or, Thank you for not being so angry today. Or maybe, Thank you for growing up. But of course she couldn't say any of it. It was too strange, the boys in her kitchen, or rather, her in the boys' kitchen, and then her increasingly elaborate fantasies about another boy that took her to a world where kitchens didn't matter.

She settled for this: "I'm glad you cut Ashleigh loose. Nothing against her, really, but I thought you could do better. Not looking forward to explaining that one to Moira, though. Moira's not the understanding type."

Devin smiled, not as big as before, but still. "Good luck. I wouldn't want to be you."

•    •    •

Her husband turned to take her hand as they made their way up the bleachers, his eyes warm and crinkled just a bit around the corners. She saw the appraising looks he got from the other women, the ones who admired his full head of curly hair and still-muscular body, all the things they wished their men had held on to a little longer. Just the night before, they'd made love not once but twice, something they hadn't done for a long time, something that made her feel exhausted and happy and guilty all at once, wondering where her appetite had come from. Lu squeezed his hand and berated herself for her own greed, for being such a man about things, for wanting her cake with a piece of Mr. Tasty Pants on the side.

Lu wished she were a man, because then she wouldn't have made the mistake of wearing hose; according to this audience, only old women wore hose. That's what Devin's mother was wearing, hose and a butter-colored linen suit. With the red hair and the red shoes, she looked like a big chicken.

"Hello, Alan," Lu said. "Hello, Beatrix. I love your suit."

Beatrix smiled and shielded her eyes from the imaginary sun glare as Lu and Ward sat behind her.

Ward shook Alan's hand and then reached for his sons, who happened to be spending that week with their mother. "Hey, sport," Ward said to Britt.

"Sport," said Britt, smiling wickedly. No matter what the situation, Britt was always smiling wickedly. "I'm so not a 'sport.'"

"What are you, then?"

"I'm a soccer god."

"Right. I'll remember that. Hey, Ollie, are you with us?"

Ollie took one hand off his Game Boy to wave at his dad but didn't look up. Ollie rarely looked at his dad too much around his mother, because it made Beatrix testy.

Beatrix got testy anyway. "You're late," she told Ward.

"Did the ceremony begin?" Ward asked.

"You know it didn't," Beatrix answered.

Ward grinned, also helpful. "Then we're not late, are we?"

Beatrix pursed her lips and faced the football field, where Devin would soon be slumping in his chair with the two hundred other graduates as the principal and the salutatorian and then the valedictorian bored everyone woozy. Lu herself was already woozy. She hated any events that required the presence of them all, hated the vapid commentary that dripped from her own lips, hated the way the boys got stiff and unsure, afraid that if they paid more attention to one parent, the other might explode in rage or, worse, tears.

The band tuned their instruments, and they all tried to pretend that they were at ease in one another's company while Lu rifled dispiritedly through her bag. That's what she did at these things, rifled through her bag. She wished that, like Ollie, she could veg out with a Game Boy, oblivious to the world. But *no,* she had to be a grown-up.

Suddenly, Ward popped up from his seat, waving at some man she didn't recognize who sat several sections below them. Before Lu had a chance to protest, Ward slipped from their row and jogged down the steps to greet him, leaving Lu to fend for herself.

She continued to rifle through her bag, furiously now. There were several things she knew: Ward was friendly, he didn't mean to make her uncomfortable, he wasn't abandoning her. And then: She should be adult enough to manage situations like these. Hadn't they been married for years? Hadn't she had plenty of practice?

Beatrix took notice of all that rifling and took pity on Lu, a frightening prospect. "Devin tells me that he applied for another scholarship through your agency."

Lu pulled a pen out of the bag, one with a wad of gum stuck to the end of it. "Well, yes. They offer a small—"

"Uh-huh," said Beatrix. "Do you know how many applications the agency received?"

"I'm not sure. It's run out of the national—"

"Right." Beatrix swiveled her head to the left and right, and Lu was again reminded of a bird, the way birds look at you: one eye at a time. "He'll probably apply for the one that Coke's doing. Oh, and did you hear about that one offered by the duct tape association?"

"No, I—"

"They want you to make an outfit entirely out of duct tape and then have someone photograph you wearing it. Isn't that crazy?"

Lu opted for the one-word answer, because it seemed that would be the only thing she'd be able to get in. "Yes."

"Devin will do it, though. He said that Ward wants him to get as much as he can from scholarships." Beatrix smiled with half her mouth. "I can believe it. You know how Ward is. Even with all his money . . ." She trailed off, shrugging, before turning around to face the field.

Shocked, Lu stared at the back of Beatrix's head and tried to figure out the most appropriate response. The options she liked most were the least mature, the least political: *thwapping* Beatrix with her purse, scrawling obscene words on her suit in red lipstick, announcing loudly that she didn't know anyone actually got gonorrhea anymore and she wished Beatrix luck with it. Her lips parted and pursed, forming words and then losing them. She thought of her old cat, Picky, dear Picky, sitting in the window, watching the birds fly past. Picky, his mouth gaping—to utter a battle cry, to protest his imprisonment, to rail at the world—and issuing only sad and silent meows.

In front of her, Alan, Beatrix's husband, fiddled with his camera case, unlocking it and snapping it shut. The curse of the second spouse: rifling and fiddling, opening and closing. She zipped up her purse and set it at her feet. Yes, she had brought baggage to her marriage, but her husband had brought the whole moving van. She imagined the graduates filing out onto the field: young and fresh and relatively unencumbered. She thought about what it would be like to be one of them, to be with one . . . say, Mr. Tasty Pants. How would he taste? Tangy. Or maybe sweet and minty, like an iced tea. And what would he do if she were to pull a whole Mrs. Robinson thing, slit skirt and shiny set hair, ice cubes clinking in a glass? She could see his face, the wide-set blue eyes even wider, the cheeks flushed, the lips parted slightly as he tried to get enough oxygen.

Ward sat down, grabbed her hand, squeezed it. She tried not to pull away, tried not to let him see her face, how far she'd gotten in the ten minutes he was gone.

"How you holding up?" he whispered in her ear.

"Fine," she whispered back, the *Graduate* vision in her head morphing into scenes of Ward crying, her mother-in-law looking at her in disgust, her stepsons frowning in confusion: What kind of skank was she?

Ward gestured at the field, where his son would soon be

tugging on the tassels of his mortarboard. "Maybe one day, we'll be watching ours," he said.

Lu felt, rather than saw, Beatrix's renewed attention, felt her cocked eyebrow like a gun against her flesh.

"One day," Lu said, patting Ward's hand.

The thing that really sucked about selling houses was all the damn paperwork. "This is what I think," Lu said. "These contracts mate with other contracts and make lots and lots of baby contracts." A sheaf of papers fell to the floor.

"Do you need me to file these?" Glynn said, appearing like an angel in front of Lu's desk, tapping a particularly precarious pile leaning like the Tower of Pisa.

"I'll take you to lunch if you file those. And dinner, and maybe for snacks later."

Glynn smiled, gathering the papers in her arms. "I like snacks." She paused. "How was the graduation?"

"Oh, you know," Lu said, remembering her own graduation, her father showing up out of nowhere with his camera, his wife, and two creepy kids, her mother pinched and furious and so quiet that Lu was afraid she had stopped breathing. "Boring speech from principal, boring speech from vice principal, boring speeches from kids number one and number two, bad choir hams up lame song with tambourines."

Glynn walked over to the filing cabinets and opened one of the drawers. "The things we do for our kids, you know?"

"Hmm . . . ," Lu said. Glynn couldn't stand her ex-husband's new wife, but she never extended the hatred to other stepmothers, something for which Lu was grateful. She liked having Glynn around the office, glad that Glynn had been desperate enough for a job that she'd jumped at the chance to be their office manager. Glynn kept Lu and all the other agents from descending into contract chaos. Plus, being a librarian, she knew things, odd facts about the average snowfall in Scandinavian countries, the mating habits of blue-footed boobies. Anyway, she was the closest thing to a real friend that Lu had made in five years, and Lu was treading lightly so that she didn't scare Glynn off.

"So what are you reading about today?" Lu asked, gesturing to Glynn's tidy desk, its pristine surface marred only by a computer, phone and message pad, and a single yellow book.

"An autistic woman."

"What?" Lu unconsciously gripped her lower abdomen, where the wrinkled eggs curled like pill bugs, shunning contact.

Glynn slipped a contract into its proper file and pushed the drawer closed. "She's high functioning, a professor of animal science. She designs equipment for farm animals, chutes and pens that help keep animals calm when they're being transferred here or there. You know what she did?"

What Lu always said when Glynn asked if Lu knew what: "No, what?"

"She observed that firm pressure calms down cows, so she made this machine for herself. You lie down in it, and these big pads compress your body, hugging you all over. She said that when she's really upset, when the world seems like a big bunch of aliens, she uses her machine, and the machine calms her."

The door to the office swung open and in strolled Mr. Tasty Pants, one hand tucked casually in his pocket. He nodded at Glynn and dropped in the guest chair on the other side of Lu's desk.

"What's up?" he said, grinning.

"Uh . . . nothing," Lu said, heart beating just a bit faster. "Did we have an appointment today?"

"Nope," he said. "But I was in the area, and I thought I'd drop by to see if we could get a look at that place you were telling me about. The one on Farwell?"

"Right," Lu said. "Right." She looked down at her messy desk, flustered. Her nose filled with his scent, light and woody and narcotic.

Glynn saved her. "Here's the listing," she said, handing Lu a flyer with a photo of a refurbished building with imposing gates all around.

"Great, Glynn. Thanks."

Glynn looked down at the golden head of Mr. Tasty Pants and then at Lu, a new knowledge in her eyes. "You're welcome."


The condo was stripped down to the studs, but they could still make out the layout, the flow. The price was right. And he would be able to choose the cabinets, the granite countertops, the bathroom tile.

Mr. Tasty Pants was pleased.

"I want it," he said.

"Well, then," Lu told him as they walked to her car and jumped inside, "we need to put a bid in right away. This is not going to stay on the market long."

He slapped his hands together, rubbed them as if he were trying to warm them up. "So, let's get back to your office."

His scent was even heavier in the small car, and her head reeled with it. "Shouldn't you call your fiancée before you make an offer on a new apartment? Won't she want to see it?"

He leaned his head back and looked directly into her eyes in the most disconcerting way, as if she hadn't a secret in the world. "I'm not married yet."

"But you will be soon."

"Soon," he said. "But not yet." He reached out and brushed her cheek lightly with the back of his hand, and she saw how very easy it would be to follow him to some motel or some apartment, fling off her clothes and her conscience, and do her best to get a string-free, full-body hug, the kind that you can get only if you can't feel too much.

"You are *so* hot," he said.

She didn't know whether to laugh or to wince. "Thanks," she said. And then: "I am married. As we speak."

He nodded but didn't drop his hand. "I know."

"You probably shouldn't be touching me like that."

He dropped his hand. "Sorry," he said, not sorry. "It didn't seem like it mattered."

"To you?"

"To you."

"Of course it matters," she said with as much indignation as she could muster. She wanted him, but she didn't want to do anything that would make people hate her. How adolescent was that?

"Sorry," he said again. "It's just that I know some women, older women, who don't care."

"Older women," Lu said, rubbing her cheek where he'd touched it.

"Sure. Even my own mother."

Lu felt a sneaking nausea. "What *about* your mother?"

"You know that saying, 'Men leave women for other women, women leave men for other lives'? My mom did that. She stepped out on my dad, found a new life. It happens."

"What are you saying?" Lu said, half-excited and half-aghast. "You want to start a new life with me? Or you think I want a new life with you?"

"Nah," he said. "I just thought you might want to . . ." He trailed off, cheeks pink. "You don't seem like the new-life type."

She closed her eyes. "Really? What type am I?"

"You want the truth?"

"Shoot."

"You seem like kind of a ballbuster." He laughed.

"Great," Lu said. "That's really great. So is the wife-to-be a ballbuster, too, or are we ballbusters just extracurricular?"

His blue eyes were earnest. "When I get married, I'm married. I'm old-fashioned that way."

Her tongue clucked of its own volition. "Marriage isn't forever, dear. Children, now *they're* forever. But marriage? Without kids? That's something you shake out and inspect every day. Like checking your shirt for stains before you put it on."

But rather than hearing this for what it was, her shredded history in a nutshell, he saw it as an opportunity. The hand was back, rubbing her cheek, her neck. "So, what's the shirt look like today?"

•   •   •

Later, she will regret that she didn't tell Mr. Tasty Pants to put it back in his pants. She will regret that she let him rub her cheek, kiss her hand for a minute or two even after he had compared her to his own *mother.* She will regret the flushed and guilty look that must have been on her face when she and the boy went back to the office, the look that had Glynn eyeing them suspiciously the rest of the afternoon. And Lu will regret that she didn't once name Ward specifically as a reason not to screw Mr. Tasty Pants brainless.

"Forget about the autistic babies," she told Annika. *"I'm* the autistic one."

"You said that the Virgin Mary would be tempted. You passed the test. And now you know you still got it."

"What do you mean, still? I *just* got it," Lu said. "And I'm losing it at the same time. How fair is that?"

"You're looking for justice? You poor thing."

"Annie . . ."

"I know, Lu. I do. But you're all right. Things are all right. It was just flirting. It was harmless. A game."

That's how she'd thought about it when she first allowed herself to think of Mr. Tasty Pants rising naked from a bathtub: harmless, just a little diversion. A person can divert themselves right out of their own lives. "I don't know what I'm doing. I don't know anything."

"You know that you don't know. That's the smartest way to be, don't you think?"

Lu didn't want to think. The more she thought, the worse she actually felt. Here she had spent so much time convincing herself that she had built something meaningful, yet she had nearly succumbed to a bit part in a slice of suburban porn. All she needed was a copy of *Madame Bovary* on the nightstand and the whole pathetic picture would be complete. *How quickly we slip and slide toward disaster,* she thought. *What sort of catastrophe would it take to teach us, finally, how and what to cherish?*

She ran, trying to imitate Vamoose, to make her body a metronome, her breath a chant, but she couldn't shut down the streaming video in her head. After Devin's graduation ceremony, the audience had wandered en masse down to the football field, searching for their offspring or the offspring of their spouses or friends. It took twenty minutes of recon to find Devin, after which everyone stood around him awkwardly, like common folk waiting for a chance to shake hands with the president. Lu wondered how Devin felt about being the center of things, about his parents' split that made him both far too important and not important enough. Devin did his best, punching his younger brothers in the arms and kissing his mother, grinning as his stepfather took photographs. He pushed away his father's outstretched hand and gathered Ward in a hug, slapping at his back. When he came to Lu, he smiled, not in the frantic and vaguely lascivious way of his middle teens, but warmly, gently. "Thanks for coming, Loop," he murmured, and kissed her, too. Watching him perform the delicate negotiations his fractured family required of him, Lu got a cramp in her throat, because she realized that she had had some tiny part in his life, even if it was a stupid part, or an annoying part, or simply a part he had to bear. And because she wished that she could love him even more for it, wished that her love weren't so mean and small and given to hiccups, like the reception on a broken radio.

*Yes,* she thought, *the radio;* she needed noise, she needed distraction. She turned up the volume so the music blared in her ears, loud enough to mask the sound of the engine that must have been revving behind her, the gaggle of boys inside working themselves up for the offensive.

When the balloon hit, when the water broke, it wasn't the blast of cold that she would have expected, but a warm torrent, like something fed and ripened by her own body, like something offered up to the world in a single bright burst. But she didn't yell, she didn't stop. She ran the gauntlet, willing to take another shot.